Sophie has been dreaming, reading and writing romance ever since she read her first Mills & Boon as part of her English Literature degree at Lancaster University.

Born in Abu Dhabi, Sophie grew up in Wales and now lives in a little Hertfordshire market town with her scientist husband, her incredibly imaginative seven-year-old daughter, and her adventurous, adorable baby boy.

In Sophie's world, happy is for ever after, everything stops for tea, and there's always time for one more page...

Claude's
CHRISTMAS ADVENTURE

Sophie Pembroke

This novel is entirely a work of fiction.
The names, characters and incidents portrayed in it are
the work of the author's imagination. Any resemblance to
actual persons, living or dead, events or localities is
entirely coincidental.

AVON

A division of HarperCollins*Publishers*
1 London Bridge Street,
London
SE1 9GF

www.harpercollins.co.uk

A Hardback Original 2016

1

Copyright © Sophie Pembroke 2016

Sophie Pembroke asserts the moral right to
be identified as the author of this work

A catalogue record for this book is
available from the British Library

ISBN 978-0-00-820205-7

Set in Sabon by Ben Gardiner

Endpaper credits: End paper illustrations
(or images) © Shutterstock.com

Printed and bound in Great Britain by Clays Ltd, St Ives plc

MIX
Paper from
responsible sources
FSC
www.fsc.org **FSC™ C007454**

FSC™ is a non-profit international organisation established to promote
the responsible management of the world's forests. Products carrying the
FSC label are independently certified to assure consumers that they come
from forests that are managed to meet the social, economic and
ecological needs of present and future generations,
and other controlled sources.

Find out more about HarperCollins and the environment at
www.harpercollins.co.uk/green

For Sam,
You are all my Christmases at once

CHAPTER
ONE

CHAPTER ONE

CLAUDE

The box on the table was filled with interesting smells. And, I guessed, interesting food that was causing the interesting smells.

I snuffled around the base of the kitchen table, wiggling my rear against the tiled floor, my tiny tail moving with it. Magnificent though I am, in dog terms, I'm just not all that tall, and try as I might I couldn't even see the box from close up, let alone reach it. I eyed the kitchen chairs. A more energetic dog might attempt to jump up, I supposed, but my legs weren't long enough to make it, and I didn't fancy the indignity of falling flat on my snout on the kitchen floor if I tried.

I *did* fancy the interesting smells, though. They smelt *delicious*.

I'd just sat back on my haunches to consider my options, when a foot collided with my side. I scampered back with a whine.

'Oh!' Daisy, one of my people, cried out as she stumbled, dropping the stack of presents she was carrying so they scattered across the table. And the floor. And one of the chairs. There was red and gold shiny paper *everywhere*. Glitter rained down from above, sparkly and shiny (but not good to eat. I'd checked).

'Claude! What are you doing there? Honestly, how do you always seem to know *exactly* the wrong place to sit? Oliver!' Daisy sounded cross. Daisy didn't often sound cross, so I made a point of listening carefully. Usually, Daisy sounded fun, and full of laughter, and like she might give me treats at any moment just for managing not to drool on her new shoes (that happened last week). But not today.

Today, I didn't think Daisy was in the mood to give me *any treats at all*. And definitely not any of the food that was making the interesting smells in the box.

This was not good.

Oliver, Daisy's husband, appeared in the doorway. He didn't look in much of a better mood than Daisy. 'What?'

'Put Claude in his crate in the car, will you? He's being *such* a nuisance.' Personally, I'd argue that the person who came into the kitchen, kicked me by accident and threw presents and glitter everywhere was much more of a nuisance. I gave a sharp bark to show my disagreement, but Daisy just glared at me. 'At least if he's in his crate he's ready to go, and it's one less thing for me to trip over in this bloody house.'

I do not like my crate. Well, it's okay for a while, I suppose. But it's not nearly as comfortable as my basket.

I turned big eyes and ears on Oliver, and hoped he was feeling sympathetic.

'Already? Shouldn't we wait until we're ready to go?' Good man, Oliver.

'We *are* ready,' Daisy snapped. Oliver gave the presents littering the kitchen a pointed look. 'Or we would be, if I wasn't the only one doing the packing.'

'I'll put Claude in the car,' Oliver said quickly, self-defence obviously winning out over sympathy. I couldn't really blame him. And actually, with Daisy in this mood, maybe I'd be safer out there anyway.

I'd be glad when all this Christmas chaos was over and

Daisy could go back to being the lovely human I knew she was. A lovely human with doggy treats, preferably. As much fun as Christmas was – with all the presents and interesting smells and lights on the tree – I didn't like how grumpy it made Daisy.

'Good. Then come back for the Christmas hamper.' Daisy waved a hand at the box of interesting smells. 'And don't forget the twins' special present! I'll get the rest of the gifts in the car, then we can round up the kids and get them loaded up too.'

'If there's still room for them,' Oliver muttered, under his breath.

I hoped he was joking. My ears had perked up a little at the mention of the kids. As much as I loved Daisy and Oliver, their children were far more fun. Especially Jay who, now he was six, had stopped trying to ride me and could play some really good games. The twins were too little to do anything much yet, but I was looking forward to watching them grow up. I hoped they'd be as much fun as Jay. Bella was older, but liked to take me for a walk sometimes – usually when she wanted to get away from her parents. She talked to me occasionally, too, curled up on the sofa when her family weren't looking. I think she liked having someone who could only bark back.

But still, I have to admit, Jay is my favourite person ever.

'Come on, Claude old boy.' Oliver hauled me into his arms and headed outside. As we passed the lounge, I saw the twinkling lights on the Christmas tree, and heard the faint sounds of the twins' favourite toy making the same noises over and over again. That was probably Jay playing with it, not them. At five months old, the twins weren't all that interested in their toys, but Jay thought they were marvellous. I'd tried chewing on one or two of them, but Oliver or Daisy always took them away.

That was okay. They didn't taste all that good anyway.

Outside, it turned out, was a lot chillier than the kitchen. The front door clattered shut behind us, the circle of leaves and berries that Daisy had hung on it thudding against the wood. The car stood on the driveway, doors wide open and the boot door up high too. It was a bigger car than most on our street, I'd realised a while ago. I supposed because we had so many more people than most of the houses on Maple Drive.

My crate sat in the boot, behind the seats where Jay and Bella sat, which in turn were behind the row with the baby seats, which were behind Oliver and Daisy's chairs. My red blanket covered the floor of the crate, and there was a chew toy or two to keep me entertained. I wondered how far we were going today.

It was Christmas, and that usually meant a few days at Granny and Grandad's house by the seaside. I liked it there – the sand was funny-feeling under my paws, and chasing the waves was always fun, even if I'd never caught them yet. But this year things felt different. Less fun, for a start. I'd been listening, while Daisy had been getting things ready for our trip, but some of the words she'd used hadn't made much sense. Ferry. France. Chateau. They were new words to me.

I had heard them talking about Granny and Grandad too, though, so that was good. It wouldn't be Christmas without them. *They* always had doggy treats for me, and their dog, Petal, was good at sharing her toys. And her people.

I didn't really like to share my people at all, but Jay loved me more than any other dog anyway, so that was all right.

I settled down in my crate as Oliver swung the door closed, and prepared to wait for the rest of the family to join me. Preferably with snacks.

It didn't take long.

'Claude!' Jay whispered my name, louder than most people would shout. I jumped up at the sound of his voice. 'I'm sorry you're stuck in your crate. I've brought you something to keep you company on the drive.' He fumbled with the door of the crate, then pushed his stuffed toy inside. I huffed my gratitude. It wasn't just any stuffed toy – it was the special French Bull-dog toy that Granny and Grandad had bought him because they said it looked just like me.

I couldn't see it, myself. My black and white colouring was far more elegant.

'Jay!' Daisy yelled from inside the house, her voice sharp and impatient, and the little boy's eyes widened.

'See you later, Claude!' He slammed the crate door shut again, running off before he could realise the latch hadn't caught properly.

Interesting.

Still, there was nowhere I really needed to go, so I settled back down with the cuddly toy for company, and watched as the family came and went, loading boxes and bags into the car, and the bigger container on the roof. Oliver staggered out with a huge gift wrapped box, bigger than my crate, and jammed it into the boot beside me. The wrapping paper had pictures of red and white striped candy canes, and golden people shaped things with sweets for buttons that looked *deli-cious*. 'Not for eating,' Oliver reminded me, as he headed back to the house for the next box. 'If you eat the wrapping paper off the twins' first Christmas present, there'll be hell to pay.'

As if I'd be so stupid. Besides, I'd tried it last month at Jay's birthday. Wrapping paper tasted only marginally better than glitter.

Every time the door opened, there was a blast of screaming from the twins. Suddenly, I was rather glad to be waiting in the car, even if no one had brought me a mid-morning snack yet.

Oliver balanced the box of interesting smells beside my crate for a moment, then placed it on the back seat instead. 'Just in case,' he said, looking at me meaningfully.

I huffed and turned around in my crate, facing away from him. No need to be insulting.

But then I spotted someone else outside the car. Someone definitely *not* family.

Perdita. The ridiculously fluffy, unnecessarily haughty, cat from across the road at number 12.

And she was sniffing.

'What's that interesting smell?' she meowed, padding closer. 'Oh, sorry, you wouldn't know, of course. You're stuck in that crate.'

Like she never had to travel in a crate to go to the vet or whatever. Cats. They always think they're better than everyone else.

'I know that whatever it is, it's not yours,' I growled back.

Perdita sprang up into the car boot, delicately climbing the mountain of suitcases and presents to reach the back seat. 'Smells like fish. Maybe smoked salmon ...' She batted the box of interesting smells with one paw.

That was a paw too far for this dog.

Without warning, I burst through the open crate door and barked at Perdita, making her yowl. She jumped backwards, away from the box, scrambling against the twins' Christmas present as she slid down out of the car. I growled in satisfaction, and she hissed back at me.

Actually hissed.

Well. A dog has his pride, right? I couldn't just let her get away with that.

I leapt down onto the pavement behind her, chasing her back down the street, away from my territory. My family.

We didn't need no stupid cats hanging around here.

I didn't intend to actually catch her, which was just as well, as Perdita positively flew across the street, up over the fence at number 12, and away. Still, I think I'd made my point.

Slowing to a stop beside a comfortable-looking patch of grass in the shelter of an evergreen hedge, I lay down to recover from my exertions. Running is not one of my favourite activities. Actually, walking is a bit much too. I like to think I was made for warming a person's feet by a fire, and eating. Puffing a little, I tried to catch my breath. I'd just rest for a moment, then I'd head back to the car. After all, I was excited to discover what ferry, France and chateau meant.

But then I heard the slamming of car doors, and the unmistakeable sound of an engine starting. And that was the moment my adventure *really* began.

DAISY

'Right. Is that everything?' Daisy buckled Lara into her car seat, ignoring her baby daughter's indignant wails drowning out the Christmas music she'd put on the car stereo, as Oliver did the same with Luca on the other side. Five months old and they already hated everything Daisy tried to do. Surely it had taken longer for that sort of objection to set in with Bella and Jay? Maybe it was because there were two of them this time. Double trouble, Oliver called them, and not without good reason.

In the row behind, Jay was trying to fasten his own seatbelt over his booster seat. Beside him, Bella rolled her eyes with the kind of disdain only a fourteen-year-old could manage, and took over, clipping it in with ease.

How had it come to this? Inside, Daisy couldn't help but feel that she was barely older than her eldest child. But out in the real world, she had four kids, a needy dog, a ridiculously large car, and a trip to make across the channel the day before Christmas Eve. Not to mention a husband who looked exhausted and grumpy before the whole adventure had even begun.

It was Christmas. A time for family, fun and celebrating, surely. Not stress eating smoked salmon from the packet and fantasising about a gin and tonic on the ferry at eleven in the morning.

'Suitcases are packed. Claude's in his crate.' Oliver ticked the items off on his fingers as he recounted the list, raising his voice to be heard over the twins' escalating cries and the sound of Slade announcing the arrival of Christmas. Still, at least the babies tended to pass out the moment the car was in motion. They just had to get on the road. Quickly. 'We have nappies, presents, snacks and passports. Anything else?'

'What about the hamper?' The same question her mother had been asking every time she'd called that morning from France to check if they were on their way yet.

'Wedged in the back seat between Bella and Jay. I figured it was safer than leaving it with Claude.'

'Good call.' Claude almost certainly wouldn't like smoked salmon, or any of the other contents of the M&S hamper, but that didn't mean he wouldn't try them, just to make sure. He'd eaten a whole bowl of cashew nuts the week before, plus a slice of cheesecake from her plate the week before *that*. She'd just nipped upstairs to check on the twins and when she got back – gone. The blasted dog was ruled by his stomach.

'Remind me why your parents couldn't just buy food in France?' Oliver asked, as he slid into the passenger seat, scowling at the fairy lights flashing on the dashboard. So she was driving then. Right.

'Apparently it's not the same.' Which Daisy would have thought was rather the point. Why move to France in the first place if you really only wanted M&S food in a slightly sunnier climate? Maybe it was for the wine. That would make sense.

'I still don't understand why we have to go at all,' Oliver grumbled, and Daisy bit the inside of her cheek to keep from responding that *he* was the one who said what a brilliant idea it was when her parents first suggested spending Christmas

18

with them in their new house in Normandy. If she'd answered the phone that night they could be eating mince pies in the peace of their own home right now.

Or possibly not. Her father could be very hard to say no to when he had an idea in his head, and as their only child she did feel a certain obligation to them. But at least *she* would have tried. Who asked their daughter to traipse across the Channel two days before Christmas with four kids and a dog in tow?

Daisy took a deep breath. It would all be fine. It would be a lovely, family Christmas. They'd all be together, playing board games, or maybe charades. She and Mum would cook a wonderful Christmas roast, and they'd all eat too much pudding. Claude and Petal would beg for turkey scraps, Jay would pull everyone's crackers for them, and the twins would sleep through the night finally.

Well, maybe not that last one. Even the season of miracles had its limits.

But the important thing was they would all be together, having precious family time.

Daisy smiled to herself. There. Everything felt much calmer now she'd focused on what really mattered. She kissed the twins in turn. They scowled back.

'Right, kids, everyone okay back there?' she called, back through the seats. No response. 'Bella?'

Daisy peered further back. Of course. Bella had her phone out and was staring intently at the screen, her headphones clamped over her ears. Jay was already deep into some game or another on his tablet. She glanced at Oliver for some parental support.

Oliver was playing Candy Crush on his phone.

Another deep breath. This one didn't help nearly so much.

'Right!' she snapped, reaching between the front seats and

whipping Oliver's phone from his hand.

'Hey!'

'Hand them over.' She held out a hand for Bella and Jay's devices, and they both stared at her in horror. 'This is a family holiday. Time for us to reconnect as a family unit. To talk, share our thoughts, play together. Not stare at individual screens for the next three days then go home again.'

'So, what? You're going to lock up our phones?' Bella raised her eyebrows. 'Seriously?'

'If that's what it takes.' Did she even have somewhere to lock them? Daisy cast her gaze around the car and spotted her mother's old vanity case that had been turned into a first aid kit, sitting on the floor of the back seat. That would do.

'But I'll miss *everything*!' Bella wailed. 'How will I know what's going on at home, with my friends?'

'You can ask them when you get back,' Daisy said. Leaning across the twins' car seats, ignoring the squeaks from the babies, she plucked the tablet and phone from Bella and Jay. Then she flipped open the vanity case and dropped them and Oliver's phone on top of the half full packets of plasters and some antiseptic cream that had gone green around the lid.

'What about *your* phone, then?' Bella's face was thunderous. 'I mean, if we're not allowed ours …'

'Fine!' Daisy pulled her own phone from her pocket and added it to the pile. She rifled around in the pocket inside the lid of the vanity case to find the key, shut the box and turned the key in the lock. 'There.' She decided to ignore the rebellious mutterings from the back seat. 'Now, is everyone strapped in?'

A downbeat chorus of agreement followed. Daisy manoeuvred herself out of the back of the car, uttering a silent prayer that the twins wouldn't choose today not to sleep in the car.

Or that they would at least stop wailing sometime soon. It was so hard to think with that constant howl of noise.

Shoving the tiny silver key in her jeans pocket, Daisy checked her watch as she reached up with her other hand to slam the car boot, blocking the noise for a moment at least. Damn, they were running late now. Portsmouth was an hour or more's drive from their leafy Surrey suburb, and the ferry wouldn't wait for them. She'd have to put her foot down to make it. Belatedly, she glanced at Claude's black and white coat through the grimy rear windscreen, small beside the absurdly huge gift she'd wrapped for the twins. What had she been thinking? Well, actually, she knew the answer to that. It had been October, and she'd still been thinking she'd be spending Christmas at home for once, instead of traipsing around the country visiting family. She'd thought that, just for once, they could have a peaceful family Christmas, just the six of them. Well, seven if you counted Claude.

She hadn't been expecting her parents' phone call with their demand that they all cross the Channel to spend Christmas in France.

Daisy sighed. It would be fine. Claude seemed to be sleeping, at least. She just hoped he didn't need a toilet stop before they reached Portsmouth ...

'Are we going then?' Oliver called from the passenger seat. From his tone, Daisy surmised that he was not best pleased to have lost his own entertainment. Well, tough.

'We are,' she said, as cheerily as she could manage. Buckling herself into the driver's seat, she started the engine and turned up the volume on the Christmas CD. 'Right. Which way do I go?'

Beside her, Oliver shrugged. 'How should I know? The sat

nav is on my phone. Which *you* locked up.'

God, he was more petulant than Bella, and Daisy hadn't honestly believed that was possible. But she was not going to let it get to her. She wasn't.

Daisy reached into the tray under her seat and pulled out the ancient road atlas they hadn't used since Bella was a baby. 'We'll just have to do it the old-fashioned way then, won't we?' she said, smiling sweetly at Oliver as she passed it to him. 'Now, who wants to play a word game while we drive? I'll start. I spy with my little eye, something beginning with M.'

'Muh! Muh! Muh!' Luca called desperately, and Lara began to wail in response.

'Misery,' guessed Bella.

'My tablet,' Jay said, sadly.

'Many, many miles of this,' Oliver muttered.

Daisy decided a few more deep breaths might be in order between Maple Drive and Portsmouth.

Not to mention a very large gin and tonic once they got on the bloody ferry.

JACK

Maple Drive might possibly be the least festive place on his post route, Jack decided, as he took in the sad, token sprig of holly tied to the door knocker of number 13. It was as if they'd all forgotten about Christmas until the last moment, then decided it wasn't really worth the bother. There was the odd wreath, a glimpse of a fake Christmas tree through a couple of windows, but that was it. Well, apart from the tasteful string of icicle lights hanging along the bedroom windowsill at number 12. And even those looked a little forlorn in the grey, pale, winter sunlight.

It wasn't that Jack thought that every house needed a light-up Santa on the roof, along with eight creepy glow-in-the-dark reindeer. Still, a little festive cheer wouldn't go amiss. He'd even taken to humming Christmas carols on his rounds, just to try and raise the street's spirits.

But apparently Maple Drive was the wrong place to be looking for cheer, festive or otherwise.

'And will you look at that travesty of a decoration across at number 12? Makes the place look like a red light zone.' Mrs Templeton, grey haired and sternly disapproving, shook her head. She reminded Jack of a head teacher he'd had when he was five, who had been scarier than all his superiors in the army put together. Who knew that returning to civilian life after ten years in the forces would still hold such opportunities to quake in his boots?

Mrs Templeton pointed forcibly towards number 12 and Jack felt obliged to look, if he had any hope of her signing for her parcel. All he could see was the delicate icicle lights under the windowsill. A small patch of brightness in the dark, winter day.

'I quite like them, actually,' he said mildly, earning himself a glare from Mrs Templeton.

'Well. I suppose you would.' She looked him up and down, and Jack wondered what she saw. Mild-mannered postman or ex-Corporal Tyler? Some days, he wasn't sure which one he was any more, either.

Mrs Templeton sniffed. 'She's pretty enough, I suppose. In a blowsy, overblown sort of way.'

Ah. That was what she was thinking. Well, she was right, to a point. The occupant of number 12 Maple Drive *was* pretty. Very pretty, in fact. But in a sad, lonely way, Jack had always thought.

And given the number of parcels he'd delivered to her house over the past few months, he'd had plenty of time to develop that opinion. Holly Starr, 12 Maple Drive, Surrey, seemed to order her entire life online, as far as Jack could tell.

'And that cat of hers! Look, there it goes now, racing about all over the place!' Jack turned to look, and saw a fluffy black and white streak flying across the road. Then, falling behind, a small, black and white dog scampering after it, his oversized ears flapping in the breeze. 'Oh, and don't get me started on the dogs on this street—' Mrs Templeton said, as the dog gave up the chase and slunk back to the pavement and, Jack assumed, home.

'If I could just get you to sign here ...' Jack interrupted, proffering his electronic pad again, and holding in a sigh when Mrs Templeton sniffed at the very sight of it.

'Modern gadgets.' She took the plastic stylus gingerly between two fingers. 'I don't know what was wrong with a pen and paper, personally.'

Jack gave her what he hoped was a patient smile. Unfortunately she seemed to take it as encouragement.

'That's what's wrong these days. Too much reliance on electronics. Especially the children. Even my grandson Zach is glued to his computer thing … but that's because his mother doesn't know how to control him. He never plays on that device in *my* house.' She pointed the stylus at him, somewhat menacingly. '*I* remember when there was none of that. Children listened and played outside in the street and they didn't act up if they knew what was good for them. And there was none of this gaudy … Americanisation of Christmas.' The stylus waved towards the icicle lights again. 'Really. Lights. On the outside of the house!'

Jack couldn't resist. 'You should see the houses on Cedar Avenue,' he said, in a conspiratorial whisper. 'One of them has a full set of Snow White and the seven dwarves lit up on their roof.'

Mrs Templeton gasped with predictable horror. 'But … that's not even festive!'

Jack shrugged. 'Well, there's also one with the Nativity. Maybe you'd like that one more.'

'I sincerely doubt it.'

So did Jack. 'Anyway …' He glanced meaningfully at the stylus, still punctuating Mrs Templeton's every thought. 'If you could just …' He shook the electronic pad again.

'Humph.' Mrs Templeton scrawled a few lines across the

screen, and Jack decided that was good enough. He handed her the parcel, along with a few Christmas card-sized envelopes on the top. She scowled at them. 'And look at these stamps! What happened to a good, old-fashioned Nativity scene for a Christmas stamp? I ask you.'

Jack quite liked the cartoon Santas, but Mrs Templeton had already shut the door before he could say so.

'Merry Christmas, Mrs Templeton,' he called, through the closed door. 'You miserable old bat,' he added under his breath.

This wasn't what he'd expected when he'd moved to Maple Drive. Fresh out of the army, he'd taken a job as a postman and, when he was assigned to an area of the suburbs with nice, neat houses, friendly looking front doors and well-kept lawns, he'd thought he'd stumbled onto exactly what he'd been looking for. Somewhere peaceful, friendly, and properly British. The sort of place he might get invited in for the occasional cup of tea or a biscuit. Or, at least, somewhere he might make new friends, and find a new community to replace the family he'd left behind when he left the forces.

He was so sure this was what he was looking for, he'd even rented one of the smaller terrace houses on the edge of the estate, just at the corner of Maple Drive.

It hadn't taken long for the illusion to be shattered.

Maple Drive might look like friendly, community-spirited suburbia, but those neighbourhood watch signs and hedges trimmed into animal shapes were misleading. The street was filled with curtain-twitchers, busy workers who left post-it notes asking him to leave their parcels in strange hiding places, and Mrs Templeton. In three months, he could count the number of actual conversations he'd had with his neighbours on one hand – and most of them had been to do with the declining standards of the postal service. He doubted anyone on Maple Drive even *realised* that he actually lived there too.

With a sigh, Jack trudged back along the street, away from Mrs Templeton's house at the top of the cul-de-sac. He dropped a few cards through the letterbox at number 11, the McCawleys', and was about to cross the street to deliver the small parcel in his bag for Holly Starr at number 12 – her of the icicles – when he spotted something shining on the driveway. Frowning, he bent down to pick it up. He held the small, silver key between two fingers and considered it. It looked like the sort of key that might open one of those padlocks that came in Christmas crackers, or maybe a secret journal or something. Probably nothing important, but still … Turning, he pushed it through number 11's letterbox to land on the cards. At least that way, they'd find it in case they needed it.

With a satisfied nod, he marched across the street to number 12. After all, it was Christmas. And the pleasure of delivering presents to Holly Starr was basically the only present he expected to get this year.

Maybe he'd even tell her he liked her icicles.

CHAPTER
TWO

CLAUDE

I scampered after the car, but being a dog of little legs, I stood about as much chance of catching it as I did of catching Perdita. Although, cars couldn't climb fences, so maybe a slightly better chance ...

Either way, by the time I got home, the car – and my family – were gone. Off to ferry, France and chateau. Leaving me behind.

Alone.

This, I decided, was simply not how things were meant to be. Ever since I was a tiny, squirming puppy, I'd always been with people. To start with, there were my litter mates, my mum, and my mum's people. Then, soon enough, there was Daisy and Oliver and Bella, and tiny Jay in his buggy. They took me home to Maple Drive, and I knew I'd never be really alone again. Oh, maybe a couple of hours when they were all out but, to be honest, in a house with so many people the occasional hour to doze away by myself wasn't a hardship. And most of the time, there was always someone around to scratch my ears, rub my belly, or refill my food bowl.

But not now. They'd packed up everything – even the box of interesting smells – and taken it with them. That meant they weren't coming back, not for a while, anyway. It was just like

31

when we went away camping (even my fluffy dog bed couldn't keep me warm that week. Jay ended up sleeping in it with me) or when we used to visit Granny and Grandad down by the seaside. They'd *meant* to take me with them, I knew. But how had they not noticed I wasn't there?

How could they have left me behind?

Me! Claude! Their beloved pet!

I hunkered down beside the bush at the end of our driveway, feeling mightily sorry for myself. I was cold and lonely and I wanted Jay. Even the twins would be welcome company right now.

Then my tummy rumbled, and I realised the situation was even more dire than I'd first thought.

I wasn't just alone, I was *hungry*. And since I wasn't meant to be there, Daisy and Oliver wouldn't have left me any food out!

I jumped to my paws and scampered up the driveway, bouncing up the three steps to the front door. I pawed at the wood and whimpered, hoping against hope that Daisy might have forgotten to lock it again and it might swing open under my paws.

No such luck.

Maybe the back door, though ... I rushed around the side of the house, but the solid wood back door wouldn't budge either. The patio doors were locked tight too and, even if I could see an open window, I couldn't jump high enough to get through them.

The house might as well have been a fortress, like the big wooden one Jay played with sometimes in his room. (I was usually cast as his noble, handsome steed. I wasn't sure what a steed was, but the noble and handsome part sounded about right.)

I sat on the back step and looked out at the garden. There

was the treehouse, if I could climb the ladder. I'd tried once or twice before, when Perdita had hidden up there, but hadn't had much luck.

Wait. Perdita.

This was all her fault. I would never have left the car if she hadn't been snooping around, trying to get into the box of interesting smells. Everything was *definitely* Perdita's fault.

Which meant it was up to Perdita to put it right. Or at least get me some food.

Daisy and Oliver and the others would be back soon, I was sure. The moment they noticed I was missing they would rush back to find me. We were family, after all, and that's what you did for family. They wouldn't leave me alone for Christmas. They'd be back in no time, probably with extra treats to make it up to me. Like the stocking they gave me last Christmas, filled with chewy treats. Yes, of course they'd be back.

I just had to be patient. And find something to eat to keep me going in the meantime.

I padded back round to the street, shivering a little in the winter air. Times like this, I almost thought Daisy had a point when she'd bought me that tartan coat. Oliver had laughed, though, so she only got it out of the coat cupboard when he wasn't looking.

Across the road stood number 12 – home of my furry nemesis. I'd never been there before, but I knew a little bit about it from previous encounters with Perdita. For instance, she'd bragged once that she had a special little door, around the back, through which she could come and go as she pleased. No waiting around to be let in or out when she needed to find a nice patch of dirt to take care of business. No waiting for her person to take her for a walk, or to tell her she had to stay inside.

Cats had the sort of freedom us dogs could only dream of. But I couldn't help thinking that they missed out on the connection we had with our people. What human really wanted a pet that didn't need them, anyway?

Usually, the fact that Perdita could come and go as she pleased, even into *my* garden, annoyed me. But today I was glad of Perdita's independence. Today, I intended to turn it to my advantage, by using her little door myself. I wasn't all that much bigger than her, and I was sure I could squeeze through if I tried. And once I made it inside …

Well, how different from dog food could cat food really be?

DAISY

Daisy let out a long breath of relief as the official gave a sharp nod, after too many minutes considering their paperwork, and let her drive through onto the ferry. Really, they were only a few seconds late. Well, maybe minutes. Certainly less than half an hour.

Oh, who was she kidding? She'd never been on time for anything since the moment Bella was born. It was as if having kids had robbed her of the ability to tell the time. Or at least to accurately estimate how long anything took. Although, to be fair, it *was* hard to predict exactly how many times the twins would need their nappies changing, or how long it would take to find whichever toy Jay had lost and desperately needed to take with him, or even how much time Bella would spend arguing about having to go out at all. She could estimate based on past experience, but somehow, whenever she thought she had a handle on it, the kids upped their game.

'Well, we made it,' Oliver said. Why did he always have to state the obvious? They could all see they'd made it. They were on the bloody boat. Funny to think that when they'd met, back at university, he'd been the one to open her eyes to all sorts of things, with his unusual way of seeing the world. The way he spotted things around them that other people would have missed. But these days … 'We're on the ferry.'

More deep breaths, Daisy. Peace and joy for the season would be a lot easier if the M25 hadn't been such a *nightmare*. Of course, it always was, and she'd known, somewhere at the back of her mind, that it would be worse today, so close to Christmas. She'd even realised, a few weeks ago, that they'd need to allow extra time for the journey because of it. But somewhere during the preparations for their trip that information had got lost in a fog of present wrapping, the scramble to write cards for all the people she'd forgotten, and the late night piecing together of a shepherd's outfit for Jay's Nativity play the following day.

Peace and joy had been in sadly short supply at number 11 Maple Drive for the last month.

'Can I have my phone back now?' Bella asked from the back seat – the first thing she'd said since losing at Twenty Questions forty minutes earlier.

'No.' Daisy didn't even think before she answered, and regretted it when the inevitable follow-up question came.

'Why not?'

Yes, Daisy. Why? Why on earth are you making this even more difficult on yourself?

She sighed. Because she wanted it to be perfect. She wanted her family to enjoy being around each other. Just for once, she wanted the stress and the constant merry-go-round of school and activities and work and nappies and emails and screens to stop. She wanted them to all just have *Christmas*, the way it used to be, when she was child.

Except in some decrepit chateau in France that her parents had fallen in love with and bought, for some reason. Some reason that probably wasn't 'to make Daisy's life more difficult' but felt like it, sometimes. Most of the time, actually.

Who really bought a chateau on a whim, anyway? Only her parents. And since they'd only moved in a few weeks ago, they'd be lucky if there were actual beds to sleep in when they got there. God only knew what sort of a state the place was in. This whole Christmas had 'disaster' stamped on it from beginning to end. Or it would, if Daisy wasn't so damned determined to drag it back from the brink of awful towards 'perfect family Christmas.' She wouldn't mind a little help with that, though.

'Because we're going to go and have dinner together on the ferry,' Daisy said, as calmly as she could manage. 'And it's going to be lovely.'

Bella gave a heavy, exaggerated sigh. Beside Daisy, Oliver gave a smaller one.

'What about Claude?' Jay piped up. 'Can he come?'

'Of course he can,' Oliver answered. 'He's part of the family, too. Right?'

'Right,' Daisy answered, wondering if the restaurant allowed dogs. That was probably something else she should have checked when planning the trip. In fact, she probably should have booked them a table. She'd thought about it, then forgotten.

Apparently fourteen years of baby brain had rendered her incapable of following a thought from beginning to—

'Urgh!' Bella wrinkled up her nose. 'Do you smell that? Is that Luca or Lara?'

Oliver grimaced. 'Both, by the stink of it. Where did you pack the change bag, Daze?'

'The change bag?' What had she been thinking about? Something to do with dinner, maybe. Well, it was gone now. 'I thought you packed that?'

'Did I?' Oliver looked puzzled. 'Maybe it's in the boot with Claude, under the twins' present.' The epically large, noisy mistake of a present. Every time they'd gone over a bump the damn thing had started singing 'Old McDonald'.

Why? Daisy wanted to ask. *Why put the one thing we're most likely to need to get to in the most inaccessible place?*

Did husbands get baby brain too? She was starting to think they might.

Oliver showed no signs of hunting down the errant change bag, so Daisy unbuckled her seatbelt and opened the car door to inspect the boot. The on-board shops would probably sell nappies and wipes anyway, right? And they had changes of clothes for the twins in the suitcase, at least. This wasn't a disaster. Calm. Peace and joy. Those were her watchwords. She wasn't going to let a little something like a missing change bag derail her festive plans. Even if it did have the twins' favourite teething rings in. And actually, possibly her purse.

No. It would be fine. It would be in the boot. Oliver was a bit rubbish sometimes, and she might not always be the most on-top-of-everything mum on the block, but between them surely they'd managed to pack a bloody change bag. Right?

Holding her breath, Daisy popped open the boot. She blew out with relief and grinned. One change bag, fully packed, sat right next to Claude's crate, only half under the Old McDonald monstrosity. See? Not so rubbish. It was all fine.

'Come on then, Claude,' she said. 'I bet you're busting for a wee, too.' She moved to unlatch the crate door, and realised it was already open. Daisy rolled her eyes. Typical Claude. Too lazy to even bother escaping when he had the option. Even now she could see through the bars that he was still sleeping!

She reached in to poke him. 'Time to wake—' Her finger

sank into the soft, plush, close cropped fur and stuffing. She blinked, gulped, and felt heat and blood racing to her head as the world started to pulse in time with her heartbeat. She needed to sit down. Or run. Or down a gin and tonic. Or all three at once, if that were even possible. 'Up,' she whispered, as the horrible truth sank in.

That wasn't Claude. The dog in the crate wasn't their beloved family pet. It was Jay's stupid bloody *soft toy*!

Panic began to spread through her veins. Suddenly, nothing else mattered – not Oliver sulking, not the twins' stupid present, not Bella's teenage strops, not Jay whining about his tablet, not even the ridiculous chateau in France they had to trek out to for Christmas. Never mind the bloody change bag. *This* was a *disaster*.

They had to get back to Maple Drive, to Claude.

Immediately.

HOLLY

Thirty-three hours and fourteen minutes until Christmas Day. Holly totted up the time left in her head, and ignored the small voice at the back of her brain that added that in that case there were only fifty-seven hours until the whole thing was over for another year, and she could go back to her ordinary life, instead of the excessively jolly, Pinterest worthy, craft and baking haze of caster sugar and spray glue she'd been living in for the last month.

She didn't want Christmas to be over. Of course she didn't. She *loved* Christmas – always had, ever since she was tiny. She hadn't lost that festive feeling even when she was a sulky teenager, or declared that 'Christmas isn't as fun as it used to be' when she became a cynical twenty-something. *Nothing* had ever dimmed her love of Christmas in the last twenty-seven years, and she wasn't about to let Sebastian bloody Reynolds ruin this one, even if it meant she had to make every single cake, biscuit, decoration and gift she had pinned on her 'Creative Christmas!' Pinterest board.

Okay, so this wasn't exactly how she'd expected to spend the first Christmas in her new home, here on Maple Drive. Back in February, when Sebastian proposed, she'd expected to be hosting family and friends for Christmas nibbles and drinks, not to mention her parents and in-laws for the big day lunch itself. She'd imagined her whole house decorated in tasteful red-and-white Scandi style, with hints of silver here and there for a little sparkle. There'd be perfectly coordinated wrapped presents under the tree. She, Sebastian and Perdita would each have their stocking hanging by the fireplace, and there'd be a personally painted family plate on the hearth ready to hold Santa's mince pie and sherry. Greenery would twine up the bannisters, twinkling with tiny fairy lights. And she and Sebastian would curl up on the sofa to watch *It's A Wonderful Life*, or *The Muppet's Christmas Carol*, and sip nice wines and eat fancy finger food and be ecstatically happy and, oh yes, *married*.

Instead, her home looked like an explosion in a kids' craft room. In a desperate effort to regain her Christmas spirit, even if she was single and alone this December, she'd thrown herself into crafting a homemade Christmas. Sebastian had always hated her hobbies – he far preferred to spend his money on the most expensive, most talked about items, and couldn't understand why Holly would even *want* to make things herself. Sometimes, she suspected that Sebastian had never understood *her*.

Holly smashed the staple gun against the 'Santa Stop Here!' sign she was making, so hard that the staple buckled and went pinging across the kitchen. She sighed. She'd have to go and retrieve it before Perdita stabbed her paw on it. Her precious – but admittedly rather entitled – cat would never forgive her.

Perdita had never really liked Sebastian. Turned out, Perdita had a point.

A knock on the door distracted her from her staple retrieval and, brushing glitter from her festively red skirt, Holly headed through to the hall to answer it, pausing only briefly to enjoy the fairy lights in the green garland on the stairs, and the tiny red felt stockings hanging from it in lieu of berries. She didn't need a husband to have a perfectly decorated Christmas, anyway. It might not be minimalist, or magazine-worthy Scandi style, but her decorations were definitely unique. And all hers.

It was, of course, the postman. Holly couldn't remember the last time anyone other than her parents and the postman had knocked on her door. And since her parents were currently cruising their way around the Caribbean, that only left one option. And as the postman was kind of hot, in a broad, dark and brooding way, she didn't mind nearly as much as she might otherwise have done.

'Another parcel for you, Miss Starr.' The postman gave her a warm smile, so at odds with the slight shadows Holly always saw in his eyes. Maybe she was imagining them. Sebastian had always said she made up stories, imagined things that weren't there. Like him being in love with her.

Except he'd *proposed*. She hadn't imagined that. He'd just changed his mind, four months later.

'Thanks.' She took the parcel from his hands and tried not to blush. Not because he was gorgeous, but because he'd been lugging at least one parcel a day to her front door for over a month now. He probably thought she was ordering them just to give her an excuse to see him. Mind you, she could think of worse reasons. Like, *I'm trying to craft the perfect Christmas to avoid thinking about how alone I am.* Yeah, she really didn't want to share that one with the postman. Although if he got a glimpse of more than her hallway, there'd be no hiding it. 'And please. It's Holly.'

'Holly,' he repeated, and her name didn't sound spiky and prickly in his mouth. It sounded warm and soft. She liked it that way. 'I'm Jack.'

Jack. A good, strong, reliable name. And he was very reliable – as a postman. Which suited Holly perfectly. An attractive man she could admire daily as he reliably delivered her craft supplies and Christmas decorations, without her ever needing to risk anything beyond a little doorstep flirting. No disappointment, no heartbreak. Just a gentle flirtation.

Perfect.

'Hi, Jack.' Holly even risked a small smile. He'd certainly earned it. Especially after last week's order of air drying clay. She'd only meant to order five small packets, but somehow ended up with five packs of twenty. They had been *heavy*.

Of course, now she had no idea what to say next. They'd exchanged names, she'd got her parcel ... what next? Did she just shut the door? Say, see you tomorrow? Make a flirty little joke? She'd never been good at this. Oh, good grief, she couldn't even manage a tiny bit of flirting with the *postman*. What hope was there for her ever getting back out there on the dating scene? None, that's what. Maybe she could craft herself a boyfriend out of air drying clay and felt.

'I like your lights, by the way,' he said, and she blinked at him in confusion until he waved a hand towards her bedroom window. Right. The icicles. She'd been a little uncertain about putting them up – no one else on Maple Drive seemed to have any – but she'd *always* had Christmas lights. Lots of them. The icicles felt like a compromise – a tiny, token demonstration of her love of all things festive.

'Um, thanks.' Now what? Did she compliment him on his postbag? What would a normal, non-craft crazy loner, do? Holly could do normal, she was almost certain. Look at the icicles!

The awkward moment stretched out between them, as Holly tried to figure out how to break eye contact. Until a sudden crash in the kitchen startled her into spinning around.

'What on earth …?' Leaving the door open, Holly dashed towards the kitchen. Maybe Perdita had found that blasted staple already. Except she hadn't heard a yowl. Perdita had a very distinctive yowl …

'Careful,' Jack said sharply, and when she glanced back Holly realised he'd followed her in. His post bag was slung over his back, and his fists were up, as if he were spoiling for a fight. 'It could be a—' They reached the kitchen, and stared at the unlikely sight before them. 'Dog?' Jack finished.

'Dog,' Holly agreed. Not just any dog. A compact, bat-eared dog that was sprawled on her kitchen floor, looking up at her with very sad and sorry eyes. The bulk of his body was white, but those oversized ears, the patches over his eyes and one or two spots over his back were black. 'He must have wriggled through the cat flap.'

'Tight squeeze,' Jack commented, eyeing the dog, then the cat flap. 'Especially with those shoulders. And that stomach.'

'And the ears …' They stood straight up, adding a good couple of inches to the dog's height, lined in a pale, velvety pink. 'What sort of dog is he, do you think?' With his wrinkled face, non-existent tail, and powerful legs, he looked like no dog Holly had ever seen before. Except, now that she thought about it … didn't the house across the road have some sort of dog? She'd never really paid much attention. She was, after all, a firmly declared cat person. Still, she was sure she'd seen the husband or the daughter walking a smallish dog from her front window, from time to time.

She'd just never studied the details. Like the ears ...

'French Bulldog, I think.' Jack crouched down in front of the creature, who was returning Holly's stare with equal bafflement. 'Hang on. He's wearing a collar. Hey there, boy.' That last was to the dog, Holly assumed, as Jack reached out, slowly, cautiously, and lifted the tag hanging from the animal's collar. 'Claude, apparently. What a name.'

'Claude,' Holly repeated. 'He doesn't look like a Claude.'

'He looks like a thug,' Jack agreed. 'Except for the ears.'

'And the eyes.' Holly frowned a little as she looked closer. 'His eyes are ... gentle. And a bit sad.' With almost the same shadows she saw in Jack's actually. The poor creature seemed to vibrate with a sense of misery. Of loneliness.

Holly could sympathise with that. Maybe she could crochet Claude a Christmas hat, or something.

'Is there an address? Or a phone number?' she asked, shaking off the strange connection with the dog.

'The McCawleys, at number 11.' Jack let the tag fall and stood up. 'So, just across the road. I think they're out though. Do you have a number for them?'

Holly shook her head. She didn't have numbers for any of her neighbours, now she thought about it. Really, they were right there, next door. That was sort of the point of them. Why would she need their phone numbers?

Besides, when she'd moved in with Sebastian, shortly after they'd decided to 'merge their lives' as he put it, she'd been too loved up and deep in their new engagement to worry about other people. There'd been decorating to do, and wedding planning, and dreaming about her future and ... and she wasn't thinking about Sebastian. Not at all.

Even if tomorrow *was* supposed to be her wedding day.

No. Back to the dog.

'I guess we could put a note through their door?' Holly said. What was the proper etiquette for dealing with house-breaking dogs, anyway?

'As long as they're not away over Christmas.' Jack straightened up and stood, leaving Claude staring up at him pleadingly.

'Do you think he's hungry?' That might explain the over-sized eyes. He looked like a creature in a Disney movie. 'Do French Bulldogs like cat food, do you think? It's all I have.'

Jack shrugged. 'It's worth a try. I get the feeling this guy might eat anything you put in front of him.'

Holly got that idea too, although she couldn't imagine where from. It wasn't like she was a dog whisperer, or anything. In her experience, animals had as much a mind of their own as humans. And God knew she'd never had much luck getting her own species to do what she wanted.

Still, she dug out a spare food bowl from Perdita's cupboard and tipped some dry food into it, laying it on the floor in front of Claude. Then, as an afterthought, she added a bowl of water. When she stepped back she realised that not only was the postman still standing in her kitchen, he was also surveying her kitchen table. Or, at least, what *used* to be her kitchen table. These days it was more like Christmas Craft Central.

'You've been busy,' he observed, reaching out to touch a string of red, gold and green bunting lying across the end of the table. The fabric shifted slightly, pulling the strings buried under the rest of the stuff on the table. Holly held her breath, waiting to see if the tower of decorations, the tangle of fairy lights or the cooling racks laden with the pieces of her gingerbread house, waiting to be assembled, would topple over at his touch. Thankfully they didn't. That was all she needed – to bury the postman in biscuits and sequins in her kitchen. 'Is this what's in all the parcels, then? Craft stuff?'

'Mostly,' Holly admitted. 'I like, well, making things. And keeping busy. Christmas is sort of the season for homemade stuff, don't you think?'

'I'd never really thought about it.' Jack tilted his head slightly as he looked at her, and Holly got the uncomfortable feeling that he was taking this new information and adding it to what he already knew about her. She just wished she knew what conclusions he was drawing. *Talented amateur craftsperson* or *crazy Pinterest addict?* Was it too much to want to know which? 'So, what was today's order? Fabric? Sequins? At least I know it wasn't more of that incredibly heavy stuff you had last week.'

'Air drying clay. Sorry.' Holly felt her cheeks warm up and knew she was blushing. 'Actually, today's wasn't craft stuff. I suspect it's Perdita's Christmas jumper.'

'Perdita?' Jack's eyebrows were raised so high they'd almost disappeared under the short, dark hair just starting to curl over his forehead.

'My cat.' Great. With two words she'd crystallised his opinion of her as a crazy cat lady. So much for trying to appear normal. Too late now, though. Holly opened the package and held up the fluffy red outfit, with brown pompoms sewn on to look like Christmas puddings.

'Ah.' Jack stared at the jumper for a moment then averted his gaze, apparently horrified. 'And does she, uh, like dressing up?'

'Not particularly.' Holly looked down at Claude, who was wolfing his way through Perdita's cat food. She wondered if he might like a Christmas sweater. 'But I feed and house her, so she has to go along with my whims.'

'Fair enough,' Jack said. 'I don't suppose Perdita is a big dog fan?'

'Not at all, I'm afraid.' They both stared at Claude who, apparently sensing the attention, sat back from the now empty bowl and stared back. 'I don't think she'd much like coming home to find Claude here. It might be a bit Goldilocks for her. You know, "Who's that eating my cat food?"'

Jack sighed. 'In that case, it looks like you're coming with me, boy.' He reached down and scooped Claude up. The dog looked even smaller, his ears even more absurd, in Jack's strong arms. At least, Holly assumed they were strong. They *looked* strong. And they'd managed the air drying clay no problem.

She might be obsessing about his arms a little bit.

'I can ask around the neighbourhood while I'm doing my rounds, see if anyone has a number for the McCawleys,' Jack went on. 'I just wish I had a lead for him. Maybe I could borrow some ribbon?'

Holly stopped staring at Jack's arms and lurched towards Perdita's cupboard instead. 'Even better. You can borrow Perdita's lead. It just clips onto the collar.' She turned to hand it to him to find Jack staring at her, for a change.

'You have a lead for your ... cat?'

Blood hit her cheeks again. Dammit, she'd blushed more this afternoon than in the past five years. 'Yes. When we moved here, she was a bit skittish. And Sebastian said ... anyway, it doesn't matter. Here you go.' No need to explain that Sebastian had said that if she couldn't control the damn animal, she'd have to get rid of it. Holly had chosen the lead as a way to try and keep Perdita comfortable and close until she settled in.

She proffered the lead again, and this time Jack took it.

'Sebastian?' he asked, as he clipped it onto Claude's collar.

'My ex,' Holly said shortly.

'Ah. Right.' Was that pity in his eyes now? Or … maybe, just maybe, was it something else?

Holly really hoped so. She was sick of pity. And perhaps it was past time for something else.

'Good luck,' she said, as Jack headed for the door. 'I mean, with Claude.'

'Thanks.' Jack flashed her a smile. 'I'll drop by later, if you like? Let you know how I get on? And return the lead, of course.'

'Of course.' Holly returned the grin. 'That would be … nice.'

'Nice,' Jack echoed.

And then they were doing the staring competition thing again, and that wasn't getting either of them anywhere.

'I'll see you later, then,' Holly said, her hand on the door. She couldn't stand around here flirting all day. She had a dozen mince pies to bake, a gingerbread house to assemble and decorate, and another lot of bunting to make.

As Jack led Claude away up the street, he turned and waved, and Holly felt that warm rush fill her again. He was coming back.

She wondered if Jack liked eggnog.

CHAPTER
THREE

CLAUDE

There is a certain indignity to being led around on a cat lead, even if no one except you and the person holding the lead knows it is one. Still, Jack the Postman didn't seem to mind the ridiculousness, so I decided I could probably bear it too.

It had to be better than wearing the hideous outfit that Holly had apparently bought for Perdita. I gave a satisfied huff. Nice to know that my nemesis cat would be facing *some* punishment after all.

Actually, meeting Holly had made me think that perhaps Perdita didn't have it quite as free and easy as she suggested. The evil fluffy cat liked to lord it over me because she could go anywhere, do anything, and was answerable to no one. But it seemed to me like Holly was rather invested in her cat – and if Perdita put up with things like Christmas jumpers, and being taken out on a lead, then maybe she was more committed to her person than she liked to admit.

It didn't make me like Perdita any more, but I was starting to believe that we were more alike than she'd been letting on.

Plus I got to eat her cat food. It wasn't as good as mine, of course, but abandoned dogs had to take what they could get.

Abandoned.

What a horrible word. I knew what happened to abandoned

dogs. Other dogs didn't like to talk about it much but, sometimes, in the park or out for a walk, you'd hear whispers. A new dog would appear on the scene, looking haunted and nervous, for instance. And someone would overhear a human muttering about owners who didn't deserve pets. Owners who beat their dogs, or starved them, or just left them somewhere, alone and scared. How this one had been lucky to find a new home. But they didn't look lucky, not straight off. To start with, they just looked terrified that it would happen again.

Over time, if they were *really* one of the lucky ones, they'd start to lose that haunted, hunted look. But sometimes they'd just disappear, and we'd never know their experiences.

And sometimes, those dogs who lasted, would talk about what happened to them.

I didn't like to listen to those stories.

And I really didn't like to think that it might be happening to me, right now.

No. I shook my head, my ears catching the wind as I trotted along Maple Drive beside Jack. I wasn't an abandoned dog. Daisy and Oliver hadn't *meant* to leave me behind, I was sure of that.

I just didn't understand why they hadn't come back yet. *Surely* they must have realised I wasn't with them by now?

'Well, old boy,' Jack said, and I stopped my fretting to listen. It's easy enough to understand humans if you're paying attention, but it's like trying to understand a squirrel or a cat. Not quite the automatic sense that other dogs make.

Well, it wouldn't be, would it? Everyone knows that dogs are the most intelligent of animals.

'Let's see if we can find someone who knows where your family are,' Jack went on, but he didn't sound like he had much hope. I didn't blame him. I couldn't remember the last time I'd seen Daisy or Oliver talking to any of our neighbours. I talked to Perdita more than they'd ever spoken to Holly, I knew that for a fact. Maple Drive just wasn't that sort of place; I didn't even know the names of some of the pets on the street. And besides, my family were always dashing here, there and everywhere, often dragging me along behind them. When would they have had time to tell anyone where they were going?

I must have looked despondent, because Jack rubbed my ears and said, 'Cheer up, Claude. I'm sure they'll be back soon, anyway. Definitely by the time I've finished my rounds, I reckon. They probably thought you were in the house when they left, right?'

I knew he was trying to cheer me up, but his words only left me more depressed. What if they weren't planning on coming back at all? They were off on their ferry, France and chateau adventure, probably having all sorts of fun without me.

Maybe Daisy and Oliver hadn't meant to leave me behind, but I was starting to worry that they hadn't missed me since they left. And what did that say about my place in the family?

The McCawleys were my pack. But to them, I was only a pet.

In which case … I looked up at Jack, who was whistling a tune I recognised from Daisy's Christmas CD. If I needed to find a new family, I could do a lot worse than Jack. He'd been kind so far, and he was helping me – even if he had put me on a lead. He and Holly had fed me, and they were trying to find my family for me.

Yes, Jack and Holly were good people. Perhaps *I'd* adopt *them*. After all, why should it always be the humans who got to choose their pets? I'd bet they'd *love* a handsome dog like me for Christmas. Suddenly, I felt a lot better about my day, and about Christmas as a whole. All I had to do was show Jack and Holly that they were my humans now. At least until Daisy and Oliver came home, anyway.

That shouldn't be too hard. Right?

DAISY

'I don't think you understand,' Daisy ground out, mentally cursing the man behind the ferry information desk. Boils in very uncomfortable places. Or maybe the tinsel that lined the desk could rise up and strangle him ... 'We need to get back to England. Immediately.'

Jay's thin arms were wrapped around her waist, clinging on for dear life, and Daisy's tunic felt damp around the middle from his tears. This was a disaster. How could they possibly have forgotten *Claude*?

'Madam, I am sure that *you* understand that we cannot simply "turn the boat around" as you say.' The official followed his words with an insincere smile that made Daisy wish for worse than boils for him. Maybe verrucas all over his face ...

Jay let out another wail, and Daisy decided to forgo the creative cursing and try begging instead.

'Please.' She looked down at his name badge. 'Henri. It's our dog, you see. He got left behind. He's all alone back there. We *have* to get back to him.'

Henri's face twisted up in disgust. 'A *dog*? Madam, these are wild creatures. They know how to take care of themselves. Really, you shouldn't worry.' He waved a hand dismissively, then selected a postcard from his clear plastic rack and passed it to Daisy. 'Here. Go treat yourselves to a free drink in our bar. Soon you will be enjoying your journey with us so much that you will forget all about your animal.'

Daisy glared at the ferry official as she took the voucher. As if a free drink could make them forget that Claude was at home, alone, scared and probably – knowing Claude – hungry.

Still, no point turning down a free G&T.

'What if it was emergency? A matter of life and death? Would you turn the boat around then?' It had to be worth a try. In fact, Daisy thought there wasn't much she *wouldn't* try right now. One way or another, they had to get home to Claude. It wouldn't be Christmas without the furriest member of their family there to share it.

'That depends,' Henri said, rather too knowingly. 'On whether the life and death in question was human or canine. Now, if you'll excuse me ...' He turned away and beckoned the next person in what Daisy now realised was a rather lengthy queue to the desk.

She sighed. Plan A was an abject failure. Time for Plan B. Grabbing another few voucher postcards from the rack when the official wasn't looking, Daisy headed off to find the rest of the family, dragging Jay along behind her.

Oliver was waiting in the bar with Bella and the twins. He already had a pint in front of him, which Daisy took as a sign he wasn't planning on driving when they reached the continent. Mind you, there were another five hours before they got there. As long as he didn't have too many more, maybe she could talk him into it.

Surely it had to be his turn to take charge for a change.

She tossed the vouchers onto the table, and sank into the plush velvet of the bench seat, Jay beside her, arms still clamped around her middle.

'Restaurant was full. But we have crisps here.' Oliver held out a packet. Daisy ignored it. 'No luck getting the boat turned around?' he asked, eyebrows raised.

Daisy's shoulders tensed. 'Feel free to say I told you so.'

'It was worth a try,' Oliver said, with a gentle shrug. She supposed even oblivious husbands had to realise eventually that there was only so far their wives could be pushed. Even if she *knew* he was thinking it inside. He'd made it quite clear how ridiculous he thought the idea of asking them to stop the ferry was. But she'd had to do *something*. Jay had been staring up at her with big wet eyes, the twins were wailing, and even Bella looked sad instead of sardonic. And just thinking about Claude … all alone, shivering in the cold, dreaming about doggy treats. It just broke her heart.

'So, what do we do now?' Bella asked. Daisy studied her daughter. Was there a hint of enthusiasm around her edges? It had been so long since she'd seen Bella enthusiastic about anything, she couldn't be sure. 'I mean, we have to go back, right? Spend Christmas at Maple Drive?'

No, that was definitely enthusiasm. But what for? Going home? Daisy could understand not wanting to go to France for Christmas – Bella had made her opinions on that idea *very* clear. But what was it about Maple Drive that made Bella want to be *there* particularly? Because heaven knew she had complained enough about home over the last year too.

There was definitely something going on with her daughter, and Daisy was determined to find out what it was. Just as soon as she'd disentangled the still sobbing Jay, fed the twins, and figured out what to do about Claude.

'But I guess that will still take a while, right?' Bella went on. 'We need to do something in the meantime. Like ... a social media campaign! Yeah, we need to start a Find Claude campaign! We could put his photo up on the internet, and get people to share it and everyone in Britain can watch out for him and report in sightings and—'

'I sincerely doubt that Claude has wandered any further than Maple Drive,' Oliver said, drily. 'In fact, he's probably still sitting on the front steps of our house.'

Bella deflated at her father's words, and Daisy glared at him.

'It's a brilliant idea,' she said, patting her daughter's hand.

Bella perked up again. 'Great! Then I can have my phone back? To start Find Claude?' Her phone. Of course. That explained everything.

'First things first.' Daisy picked up the vouchers and handed two to Bella. 'Get me a Diet Coke, and an apple juice for Jay, please?' The gin and tonic would have to wait, unfortunately.

Bella rolled her eyes, but at least did as she was asked. Daisy decided that this was progress.

'So,' Oliver said, handing Jay a napkin to wipe his nose on. 'What *do* we do now? Put out some sort of tear jerker video through the major news outlets, telling Claude that we're not angry, we just want to know that he's safe?' Daisy ignored his sarcastic tone.

'We *do* need to make sure that Claude is safe,' Daisy said, thinking aloud. 'She's right about that. Perhaps we could call home to one of our neighbours? Ask them to look out for him?'

'Do we even have any of our neighbours' numbers?' Oliver frowned. 'Honestly, I can't even remember most of their names.'

'Well ... I think I might have Mrs Templeton's in my phone somewhere. From that neighbourhood watch thing she tried to rope us into.' Obviously, it would be better if she had someone else's number – anyone else's number – but this *was* an emergency.

'Do you really think that Mrs Templeton is going to go out hunting for Claude then feed him dog biscuits until Boxing Day, just because we asked? She's not exactly Claude's biggest fan, you know.'

'Or ours.' Somehow, Mrs Templeton always seemed to be around when Claude or one of the kids was doing something they shouldn't be. Daisy half thought that the old bat spent her days peeking around her curtains waiting to catch them in the act. She sighed. 'I don't see that we've got much choice. We don't know anyone else, and we can't leave Claude all alone there. Maybe if we explain that we're going to head back as soon as we can, she might agree to help us out?'

'Are we?' Oliver asked. 'So we're canning the whole idea of Christmas at your parents' new "chateau"?' He put air quotes around the last word. Daisy had a feeling he wasn't expecting much from his in-laws' latest property purchase. Not that she blamed him. She was expecting mice and potentially crumbling masonry.

'I think we have to, don't you?' Daisy said. 'We can try to get seats on the first ferry back. I'll call Mum and Dad and explain. I'm sure they'll understand.'

Oliver looked rather less convinced, but really, what else could they do? 'Okay then, so the first thing is to retrieve the phones. Give me the key?' That, at least, Oliver seemed pleased about. Even Jay perked up for a moment at the prospect of getting his tablet back.

'Fine,' Daisy huffed. Reaching into her jeans pocket, she felt around for the tiny silver key she *knew* she'd put there.

Nothing.

As Oliver watched with a look of mounting horror, Daisy pulled out a stack of used tissues, a rogue dummy, a receipt from the petrol station, two jelly babies and a glittery green bow from the top of a present.

But no little silver key.

'Maybe there's a pay phone?' she said, hopefully, as Oliver's forehead clunked against the table.

JACK

Jack couldn't remember the last time he walked a dog. When he was growing up, they'd had dogs as family pets – usually something of a decent size, like a Labrador or a Border Collie. Never anything as small as Claude. But the last dog had passed away not long before his dad followed his mum up to heaven, just after Jack enlisted, and since then ... well, the army life-style hadn't been very conducive to pet ownership.

He glanced down at Claude, trotting along beside him at the end of the sparkly pink lead, his oversized black ears perked up and listening to the world around them. Maybe he'd check if his rental agreement could be amended to allow pets. He knew at the moment they were forbidden, but perhaps that could be fixed. Or if he moved ...

He'd already put an email in to his boss to see if it might be possible to get a transfer. Maple Drive hadn't lived up to his expectations at all. No point hanging around to see if things changed; they never did, in his experience. No, it was time to move on and start looking elsewhere. But in the meantime, maybe a dog would give him the companionship he craved.

A proper dog, though. One with a decent tail for wagging, and less obtrusive ears.

'Well, I guess we'd better see if anyone around here knows

where your owners are, boy.' Great, now he was even talking to the dog. *That's* how hard up for human connection he was.

Except … he'd connected with Holly. At least, he thought he had. It had been a while since he'd felt that sort of connection with, well, anyone. Perhaps he'd been imagining it. Perhaps she'd just been thinking 'Who is this strange man in my house?' As well as 'Who is this strange dog?'

All in all, it had been a strange encounter all around. Although that didn't mean he wasn't already humming with the anticipation of seeing her again later.

But first he had to finish his round. And find something to do with Claude, who was sticking very close as he trotted alongside.

'I just hope someone in one of these houses knows how to get in touch with Mr and Mrs McCawley.' Who knew what he'd have to do with Claude otherwise. Claude moved a little closer again, almost tripping Jack over, as if he had the exact same fears. Maybe he did, Jack allowed, as he did a little hop-jump to avoid getting tangled in Claude's lead. Nobody liked to be left alone, after all.

Jack knew that feeling. Except he hadn't been left, exactly. He'd chosen to leave. He had to remember that.

The first couple of houses they came to were dark. Jack knocked on the doors anyway, as he pushed their Christmas cards and bills through the letterbox, but there was no answer. The next door was opened by a harried-looking young woman with a baby in her arms, and Jack brightened. This house had to be a better shot. After all, if the mum was home with the baby, surely she'd have more contact with the rest of the community.

'Hi, I was wondering if you could help me. I'm trying to get hold of this little guy's owners. The McCawleys. At number

11.' Jack kept a friendly smile on his face throughout, but it didn't seem to register. The woman shook her head, grabbing the small pile of post from his hand without even glancing at Claude.

'No thanks,' she mumbled, as she shut the door.

Jack sighed. He'd known that finding someone who knew the McCawleys well enough to be able to fill him in on their movements was a long shot, but he hadn't expected it to be so hard to even find someone willing to listen to him.

As he trudged back up the driveway, grateful for his winter coat in the bitter December cold, his phone rang. Jack fished it out from his pocket, while Claude danced around his feet, wrapping the lead around his ankles.

'Hello?' Jack said, carefully stepping out from the tangle of lead again.

'Jack? It's Bill.' His boss. Jack tensed. Even though he knew this probably had to do with the email he'd sent Bill last night, there was always the chance that it was something worse. But then Bill said, 'About this email,' and Jack let himself relax, just enough to head to the bus shelter at the end of Maple Drive and sit down while they talked. Claude entertained himself sniffing around the base of the bench legs, before curling up on Jack's boots.

'Yeah. What do you think? Is it possible?'

'A transfer? Yeah, I guess so. Probably. It might take a while, but … to be honest, Jack, I'm more interested in why you want one.' Bill sounded personally affronted. Maybe he should have gone and talked to the guy in person, instead of just emailing. It was just that it had been late, he'd been frustrated, and he'd wanted to do something – anything – to feel like he was moving forward again.

'It's nothing to do with you, or the job,' Jack said quickly. 'Honestly, I'm happy working here. Very happy.'

'Except for the part where you want to leave,' Bill commented. 'So again, I have to ask … why?'

Jack sighed. How to explain it? 'I guess … you know when you have an idea of how things are going to be? What your life will be like when you reach a certain point, a certain place?'

'Yeah. Sure.'

'Well, I thought being here, living on Maple Drive would be … different.'

'Different how?' Bill asked.

That, Jack knew he couldn't explain. Maybe to someone else – someone like Holly, perhaps. But not to Bill – gruff, contented Bill. Bill had lived in the local area all his life, he'd told Jack proudly on his first day, and worked for the post office since he left school. Bill had his children, his grandchildren, his siblings, his nieces and nephews, his cousins, and every school friend that ever mattered to him, all living within a twenty mile radius. Bill didn't just live here. He belonged.

And Jack hadn't belonged anywhere since he left the army. But he was determined that he would.

It just seemed that Maple Drive wasn't the place for belonging. Nobody wanted anything to do with each other, as far as he could tell. And that wasn't the sort of place that Jack wanted to call home.

'I thought I could make this place my home,' he said, at last. 'But I think maybe I'd have better luck somewhere else. I think it's time for me to leave. Move on, you know?' At his feet Claude looked up, his eyes huge and his oversized ears strangely droopy, as if he understood every word Jack was saying and didn't like it one bit.

Bill sighed down the line. 'Son, I've not known you all that long, and I wouldn't presume to try and guess your life story. But I know you were in the army, and I reckon that probably meant moving around a lot, right?'

'Right,' Jack said, wondering where the older man was going with this.

'And now you're looking to put down roots,' Bill went on. 'But the thing is, roots take time to grow. They need to settle in, get comfy like, before they can stretch out and really take hold in the dirt. It's like the weeds in my allotment. If I get hold of them quick, when they've just arrived, they come up easy as anything. But if I let them stay too long …'

'They take root,' Jack finished for him. Was that what he needed to do? Take root? Maybe … but not in Maple Drive.

'Exactly. But it does take time. And if you just up and leave every time something doesn't seem quite like you expected, well, you might never get those deep, strong roots you're looking for.'

'So you're saying no to the transfer.' Maybe Bill had a point. But as Jack looked around Maple Drive – at the darkened windows, the empty driveways, the locked front doors – he couldn't help but think that none of the other people living on the street had real roots either, no matter how long they'd lived there. Why would he be any different?

'I'm saying think about it some more, that's all,' Bill said. 'It's Christmas Eve tomorrow, son. At least give it until the New Year.'

That was fair, Jack supposed. After all, he'd already been there for months. What was another couple of weeks?

'Okay. But if I still want to leave then?' Which, as far as Jack was concerned, was a dead cert. Claude shook his little head and got back up on all fours, padding over to the edge of the bus shelter, pulling his lead taut.

'Then I'll fast track your transfer myself,' Bill promised. 'Deal?'

'Deal.'

'Good. Now get on with your round.' The phone line went dead, and Jack smiled as he slipped his phone back into his pocket.

Bill was right; he had deliveries still to make. And a dog's family to find – even if it already seemed like the McCawleys were another family that didn't have roots here in Maple Drive, he still had to try.

'Come on, Claude,' he said, tugging the dog away from the corner of the bus shelter, where he'd found something very smelly to investigate. 'We're not done here yet.'

CHAPTER FOUR

CLAUDE

The afternoon was fading into evening before Jack had finished making his rounds. Turned out, he didn't just deliver post on our street, but *all* the streets surrounding them. Once we'd tried all the houses on Maple Drive that had humans at home, he'd taken me on the rest of his round, promising we'd come back and do the rest later, when more people were home. My paws were aching, and I was thinking longingly of my cosy basket and my red blanket. Or even Perdita's food bowl, for that matter!

But more than anything, I was thinking that Jack was leaving too. I'd heard every word of his phone call, even if he hadn't known I understood. He didn't want to stay in Maple Drive.

Just like Daisy and Oliver, he'd be leaving me behind.

'Not too many more now, boy.' Jack bent over to rub between my ears, which I appreciated. At least he seemed pleased to have me around for now.

The other occupants of Maple Drive had been less keen.

I'd expected it from the humans. I'd noticed in the past that while people could be very attached to their own pets, sometimes they were less fond of other people's. That certainly seemed the case in Maple Drive. Of the four houses that had people at home, only *one* had reached down to pat my head. One! The others had hardly looked at me. Except for the one who said something very rude about my ears.

The worst part was, none of them knew where Daisy, Oliver and the children were. And I couldn't explain ferry, France and chateau to them.

Still, I'd hoped that I might have some luck with the other animals on the street. I figured that they, at least, would be sympathetic to my plight. And maybe one of them might know about ferry, France and chateau. Even better, with Jack leaving, maybe one of them might be able to take me in. Just in case my people didn't come home anytime soon.

There were more pets on Maple Drive than I'd realised, actually. Some of them I'd seen around before – some of the cats I'd even chased out of my garden. But I'd never really had a proper conversation with any of them before today.

At one house, I met a spaniel, who bounced towards the door, ears flapping with great excitement, until his owner grabbed his collar. While Jack recited his question about my owners again, I barked a quick, quiet question of my own to the spaniel. 'Is this a good home?'

The spaniel's response was typically enthusiastic. 'It's the best! I love it here! There are treats and scratches and tummy rubs *all the time*!'

I looked up at his owner again. He seemed okay. And if the spaniel was happy there … I turned my most appealing look on the man, and waited for him to look down and notice. Because, of course, it wasn't up to the pets who got taken in. That came down to the owners.

The man glanced down at me, brow furrowed.

'Sorry, mate, I don't really know them,' he said, turning his attention back to Jack. 'Don't even remember seeing that dog around the street. And I'd definitely remember those ears!' He laughed, and Jack laughed with him, so I resolved to tangle the lead around his ankles again sometime soon.

My ears are *magnificent,* thank you. Daisy says so.

It was the same story everywhere we went. Everyone nodded and said, 'Hmm, yes, number 11 …' but in the end, they had to admit they didn't know Daisy and Oliver at all.

Inside every house, I saw glimpses of Christmas trees and lights shining, happy smiles and delicious smells. But none of it spilled outside their houses, out into Maple Drive. And none of it was for sharing with a poor, lost and abandoned French Bulldog.

I tried my luck with another dog – this one a much calmer Westie, who seemed apologetic, at least, for her owner's comments on my appearance – and two cats. Unfortunately, both the felines were members of Perdita's little gang, and one of them had scraped their back leg last time I chased them over the fence, so that was that.

The McCawleys and I officially had no friends in Maple Drive.

Well, except for Jack. I had Jack, for now, at least.

He'd told the man on the phone he'd think about it – think about whether he really wanted to leave? Probably. In which case, all I had to do was find a way to convince Jack that Maple Drive was worth staying for. None of the people we'd spoken to that afternoon had helped with that *at all.* But this morning … Holly had let him into her house, had welcomed him, talked with him.

Maybe that was a start. Maybe we just needed more people like Holly to talk to.

Because one way or another, I had to find Jack a reason to stay here on Maple Drive. Otherwise, I had no idea who would look after me.

DAISY

The ferry lurched port-wards (or was it starboard? She never could keep those straight) and Daisy clung onto a row of chairs to keep her balance. Oliver and the kids were still bemoaning the lack of electronics while eating crisps in the bar, so Daisy had volunteered to go and find out about getting a seat on the next ferry home. She had a nasty feeling it might be an overnight crossing, and if they ever managed to get a table in the restaurant, she suspected they might not all keep their food down until they reached Portsmouth again.

There you go. A good reason to be grateful she hadn't booked a table in the restaurant.

Mind you, no one seemed to be grateful about anything else. And yes, okay, she hadn't pulled off the smoothest family holiday ever so far on this trip, but she *had* put a lot of work into it, whatever Oliver seemed to think.

She'd booked the ferry, ordered the M&S hamper, packed everybody's stuff, bought and wrapped all the Christmas presents (well, most of them. There was still a bag or two of gifts in need of wrapping when they were somewhere that didn't sway quite so badly) *and* decorated the damn house, even though they weren't there to enjoy it.

She had *done* Christmas, and it wasn't even Christmas Eve yet.

Still, if they could just get back to Maple Drive, back to Claude, and have a nice Christmas day with turkey and crackers and slobbing on the sofa watching a bad movie, it would all be worth it.

Daisy joined the queue at the information desk again, hoping against hope that whoever was manning it now would be more sympathetic than the idiot who wouldn't turn the boat around.

No such luck.

'Ah, Mrs McCawley, isn't it?' Henri smiled insincerely at her. 'I *do* hope you enjoyed your free drinks.'

'Not really. Listen, I need to book passage for my family on the next ferry from Caen to Portsmouth. Can you do that for me?'

'Of course!' he said, and Daisy's spirits started to drift slowly upwards, in the manner of mulled wine steam. Until he added, 'Normally. But not today.'

'Why not today?' Daisy ground out, wishing she had a vat of steaming mulled wine to pour over the odious man.

'The seas, in case you failed to notice in your all-encompassing worry for your *dog*, are rather rough today, madam. All sailings after this one have been cancelled, until tomorrow morning.'

Tomorrow *morning*? That meant leaving Claude all alone overnight. They'd never done that before, not anywhere. He'd always come with them – every family holiday, every weekend away, even an overnight stay. The most he'd managed was a few hours with her parents one evening.

What was he going to do? Daisy hoped against hope that Claude had managed to sneak back into the house without them noticing – it seemed the most likely reason for his escape, wanting to get back to his comfy basket, or his food bowl.

But what if he hadn't? What if he was all alone, hungry, and outside in this dreadful winter weather?

What would he do?

'But tomorrow's Christmas Eve,' she whispered.

'Very observant of you, madam,' Henri said, crisply.

'But you run ferries on Christmas Eve?' It wasn't ideal, but if it got them back to Claude ...

'One ferry,' he corrected her. 'At 8.30 a.m.'

'Well, can you book us onto that one?'

'Of course!' This time, Daisy knew better than to let her spirits rise. 'Usually.'

'Usually,' Daisy echoed. 'But not today.'

'But not today,' Henri confirmed. 'I'm afraid tomorrow morning's sailing is very popular – and fully booked.'

'Is there a waiting list?'

'A long one.'

'Can you put us on it?'

'I suppose so,' he agreed, grudgingly. 'But personally, I don't think you stand a chance.'

'It's Christmas,' Daisy said. 'The season of miracles.'

'Forgive me, but do miracles usually involve sea-going passage? Unless you're planning on walking on water, of course ...'

'Just put us on the list,' Daisy snapped.

Henri obliged, taking down her parents' phone number in France – which Daisy fortunately had scrawled on the back of a receipt in her purse from when they'd called – and promising that someone would ring them if places became available on the ferry.

'Now, if I can be of no further assistance ...'

'I think we're done here,' Daisy agreed, but before she could step away, she heard Bella's voice.

'Mum!' Bella bounded up beside her, smiling at Henri. 'Did

you get us on the ferry?'

'No, she did not,' Henri answered, before Daisy could find a gentle way to break the news to her daughter. She scowled at him, and wished him a plague of Christmas tree needles somewhere very uncomfortable.

Bella frowned, and shook her head. 'In that case, we need to get Find Claude up and running as soon as possible. If we're not going to be back tonight—'

'Excuse me. Find Claude?' Henri asked.

'It's a social media campaign to try and find our dog,' Bella explained.

'Of course it is.' Henri's voice dripped with disdain.

'It's a genius idea,' Daisy said, wrapping an arm around Bella's shoulder, which Bella promptly shrugged off.

'Did you find the key yet? So we can get the phones out?' Bella asked.

'Not yet,' Daisy admitted.

'It's astonishing how careless people can be with personal belongings,' Henri added, unhelpfully. 'Like keys. And dogs.'

'You must have computers with internet on this ferry, right?' Bella leant further over the counter, staring at Henri, and he took a step back. 'Where are they?'

Henri, stunned into helpfulness, gave them a map with the internet hub marked. Daisy trailed after Bella as she strode towards the computers.

'So, how is this going to work, exactly?' she asked, as Bella settled in front of the screen.

'Easy. I'm going to set up a page called Find Claude, right?' She was already typing away, the screen filling with text and images as she worked. 'I'll link it to my profiles and share it with my friends, and get them to share it with their friends and so on and so on.'

'Until everyone we've ever met knows we're negligent pet parents who left their dog at home.' How exactly was this going to help?

'Until even people we've *never* met are helping to search for Claude.' Bella tapped a few more keys, and a picture of Claude from last Christmas, wearing a Santa hat perched between his dark ears, appeared at the top of the page. 'And done!'

'That was … amazing.' Daisy scanned the screen. She liked to think that she was pretty good with computers, but she wouldn't have thought of this. All she'd been thinking about was finding a way home. But since she couldn't, Bella had done the next best thing.

Find Claude! the page read, in big letters, under Claude's picture. Beneath that Bella had written a paragraph about what had happened that morning. Then she'd started adding friends to the page, and sharing it everywhere.

'So, now what do we do?' Daisy asked, as Bella logged off the computer.

'Now we wait for people to contact us and tell us they've seen Claude.'

'Great.' Waiting. Daisy's favourite.

'Don't worry, Mum.' Bella squeezed Daisy's hand with her own. 'Claude will be fine.'

'I hope you're right.' Because, whatever she did, they weren't going to get home before Christmas Eve. Which meant that Claude would be all alone tonight – and probably hating every minute of it.

It seemed that Bella's Find Claude campaign was their best chance of taking care of their favourite dog, even if they couldn't be there themselves.

HOLLY

By the time the sun had set – at, admittedly, the ridiculously early time of four o'clock – Jack still hadn't returned with Claude.

Holly had made two batches of mince pies (one with ordinary mincemeat, one with her speciality cranberry and apple one), assembled the pieces of her gingerbread house ready for decorating, prepped a batch of mulled wine (eggnog was, after all, more of an acquired taste, and she didn't know if Jack had acquired it. But surely *everyone* liked mulled wine), sewn another string of festive bunting, and dug her second set of icicle lights out of the spare decorations box.

She'd held off putting them up before now, because Maple Drive didn't seem all that big on Christmas lights, and as the only one indulging in the festive display she didn't want to overdo it. But it was Christmas Eve tomorrow and Jack *had* said he liked them, so maybe one more string, just under the dining room window, wouldn't hurt.

Besides, they looked cheery whenever she came home, like the house itself was welcoming her. She liked that.

Slipping on her bright red coat, Holly picked up the coiled string of lights and headed out the front door, smiling at the sight of her sparkling bauble wreath as she did so.

She attached the battery pack as instructed to the side of

the window, then set about draping the icicles as evenly as possible under the windowsill.

'What on *earth* do you think you're doing, young lady?' Holly froze at the sound of the voice behind her, then turned slowly to check there wasn't some other twenty-something blonde being berated for her behaviour.

Nope. Just her.

At the end of her path stood the fearsome Mrs Templeton from number 13, hands on her hips, scowling furiously.

'I'm ... putting up Christmas lights?' She was pretty sure that's what she was doing, anyway. From Mrs Templeton's tone, though, she might as well have been setting up a brothel in her front room.

'In case it has escaped your attention, Maple Drive is not the sort of street that encourages Christmas lights.' She spat out the last two words as if they tasted bad.

And in case it escaped your attention, this is my house and I can do whatever I like to it.

She should just say that. It was true, after all, and it wasn't like the street *belonged* to Mrs Templeton or anything. And hadn't she decided to be more herself, and less the Holly that Sebastian had wanted her to be, now he was gone?

But this was her home. And maybe it wasn't the way she'd planned, when she'd moved here with Sebastian, but in some ways that just made it even more important to fit in. She was alone here now. If Mrs Templeton rallied the neighbours against her, they could make her life miserable. Run her out of town, even! All over a set of Christmas lights.

Holly shook away images of her neighbours chasing her with flaming torches, and concentrated on placating Mrs Templeton.

'I'm sorry you don't like them,' she said, sympathetically.

'But really, it is just one very small string of plain white lights.'

'Two strings.' Mrs Templeton nodded towards the bedroom window lights. 'Two strings of wholly unnecessary lights.' Holly winced.

'But don't you think they brighten the place up a bit?' she tried. After all, wasn't that basically the job description of lights? Brightening things up? Even Mrs Templeton couldn't argue with that, surely?

'I think they make the street look tacky.'

Right. Of course she could.

'I'm very sorry you feel that way,' Holly said.

'So you'll take them down?' Mrs Templeton's scowl didn't lift for a moment.

Holly sighed. Maybe she should try appealing to the woman's humanity. If she had any. 'The thing is … I live alone here, apart from my cat. And that can get rather … lonely. And the lights, well … it's just nice to have something to welcome me home during these cold winter nights. Even if it is just battery-powered,' she joked, then smacked a hand over her mouth at the thought, as the innuendo caught up with her. Oh, why couldn't she just *stop talking* before she got to the embarrassing parts?

Mrs Templeton took a moment longer to catch on, but then her eyes widened and her mouth opened into a tiny, tight O shape.

'Well,' she said after a second. 'Well, I'm sure it's none of my business *what* you get up to in the privacy of your own home, but out here on the street I am still the neighbourhood watch captain for Maple Drive, and I say that those lights have to go!'

'Right. Of course. Sorry.' Her cheeks burning, Holly ripped out the drawing pins holding the lights in place, and started coiling the string back up. 'I'll take down the upstairs ones now.'

'Good. Right.' Mrs Templeton turned on her heel and marched away, pausing at the join between Holly's front garden and hers to cast back a suspicious look. Holly sighed. So much for trying to fit in. Before she knew it, Mrs Templeton would be telling the whole street that Holly Starr really *was* opening a brothel in her front room.

Lights in hand, Holly headed inside, slamming the front door behind her. She stomped up the stairs, opened her bedroom window wide, and began gathering in those lights as well.

Then, surrounded by icicles, she sat on her bed and tried very hard not to cry.

This had been a mistake. All of it. Meeting Sebastian in that blasted bar and falling for his charm. Moving to Maple Drive with him and buying the house when they'd only been together less than six months. Deciding to stay here even after Sebastian left. Telling her parents that *of course* she didn't mind if they spent the money they'd got back from her wedding insurance on a Caribbean Christmas cruise instead, since she 'wasn't going to be needing it.' God, she'd even reassured them that she'd be okay on her own for Christmas. That she had friends she could spend it with, and hoped they didn't ask for their names, since she didn't think Perdita would be an acceptable answer.

But most of all, Sebastian. He was the biggest mistake she'd ever made in her whole stupid life, and he was still making her miserable, four months after he left.

Sebastian would have hated the icicle lights too. And Perdita's Christmas jumper. And mulled wine.

Really, she'd had a lucky escape. All that time she'd wasted imagining her perfect future with him, not realising that they had nothing in common, that everything she dreamt about he'd have shuddered and turned his nose up at.

He didn't even like *Christmas*.

Really. She was *so* much better off without him.

Except that without him meant being alone.

Holly stared at the sad strings of unlit icicles lying against her duvet cover. Inside, without their little bulbs gleaming, they were useless. Surplus to requirements. Just like she'd proven to be to Sebastian.

The thing is, Hol, I thought I wanted to get married. Really I did. I mean, they say that's the best way to get up to the next level at the company – show that you're serious and all that. But now I've got this new job offer over in Dubai ... Well, we don't need to any more, do we? And you'd hate it over there. Far too hot for you. You'd burn in minutes. So maybe it's just best for both of us if we call it a day. Don't you think?

Best for both of them. Like he was doing her a *favour* walking out on the life she'd imagined for them.

But since it turned out that all he'd wanted her for in the first place was a promotion ... Holly shuddered. Lucky escape. She really had to concentrate on that part.

How had she not seen it sooner? Maybe she was just a rubbish judge of character.

It wasn't being without Sebastian that bothered her most, though. It was wondering if she'd ever get another chance to do it right.

Well, she knew one thing. Hiding away in her bedroom, crying over sodding icicles, wasn't going to get her anywhere. And neither was apologising to Mrs Templeton, and letting the old bully dictate where she could and couldn't hang her lights.

This was *her* house. Just hers, now that Sebastian had

gone. She worked damn hard to keep up the mortgage on her own, supplementing her teacher's salary with the income from her online craft shop, and cake orders from friends and family. She deserved to decorate it any damn way she pleased.

And what pleased her right now was bright. And gaudy. And everything else Mrs Templeton hated.

Hell, she'd hang light-up vibrators from the bedroom window right now if she had them.

Well, maybe not that. But she *did* have a priority account with next day delivery at a really fab online decoration store …

It was time to move on – from Sebastian, and being the sort of woman who said yes to a man who only wanted her to further his career. From being the Holly he walked out on, leaving her feeling that *she* hadn't done enough to keep him.

That was bollocks.

She was ready to be herself again – the Holly who loved Christmas, who *made* things rather than buying them, who dressed her cat up and took her for walks on a sparkly pink lead sometimes.

Sebastian hadn't deserved her. She didn't need him, and she didn't even need her parents here to coddle her through her first Christmas alone. They deserved their own life, too. She'd rather be alone, being herself, with a chance of one day finding someone who loved her for who she really was, not in spite of it. Because, actually, she was kind of awesome. And one day, someone was going to realise that. And until then …

It was time for Holly Starr to sparkle again.

Starting with the icicles.

She was going to hang them from every window on the front of her house. And then she was going to go online and order lawn decorations. Because this was her Christmas too – and she was doing it her way.

CHAPTER
FIVE

CLAUDE

'Last house,' Jack said, looking down at me sympathetically. We were back on Maple Drive, at least; I could see my home across the road. In fact, the house Jack was heading for was just next to number 12. 'Then we'll go back and see Holly. Get you off this lead.'

Thank goodness for that. My dignity had reached a new low, being paraded around with pink sparkles around my neck. Not to mention the fact that my paws were smarting from so much walking.

I am not, typically speaking, much of a 'walking' dog. A quick stroll once or twice a day suits me just fine. Not several hours delivering mail all around the county.

Still, this last house had potential. As we approached the front door, interesting smells floated out to greet us. And when Jack knocked and the woman inside opened the door, the smells only grew stronger.

I'd never smelled smells like these before. These were even more interesting than those inside the box of interesting smells that got me into all this trouble in the first place.

I had to know what they were.

The woman who opened the door was older than most of the people on Maple Drive – older than Mrs Templeton,

89

even. Her dark grey hair was short around her ears, and her face lined a bit like mine. Her eyes were tired and a little sad. Under all the interesting aromas coming from her house, I thought I could smell a kindred spirit – someone as lost and lonely as me this Christmas.

Clearly, it was my duty to keep her and whatever those brilliant smells were company.

I waited until Jack reached into his bag to pull out a parcel, knowing that at that moment he had to loosen his hold on my lead for a second while he juggled packages and the strange electrical device that people had to write on.

With exquisite timing, I tugged free, weaving through the woman's legs and darting towards the interesting smells with what I imagined might be the last of my energy.

Well, if I had to collapse with exhaustion, I just asked that it be within tasting distance of those smells.

This house was the same layout as mine, and as Holly's, but it felt very different, even from the doorway. There were no Christmas decorations up for a start that I could see – not even a tree towering in the hallway like at ours. (Daisy had spent a whole evening hanging shiny things on it, then wouldn't let me play with even the little ones I could reach at the bottom.) But there were other things – ornaments and other types of shiny things set out on every shelf and ledge. Jay would have knocked all of those off with just one quick game of Flying Zebra, the mix of catch and fetch he'd invented to us to play with one of the twins' many soft toys.

The smells weren't coming from the ornaments, though. I dashed through the hallway before Jack or the woman could stop me, and towards where I knew the kitchen would be. Kitchens are always good for interesting smells.

This kitchen table was a little lower than ours, and had a bench that even I could clamber up onto. With my hind legs on the bench, I placed my front paws on the table and breathed in deeply. *Those* were the smells I'd been looking for all my life. I didn't know what they were, but I wanted them. Badly.

'*Claude!*' Jack's voice was stern, and my ears flattened a little against my head. I had a feeling I might have been a bad dog.

'I'm so sorry, Mrs Nordmann,' Jack said, following the woman into the kitchen. 'He's not actually my dog. I'm just looking after him for the day, until we can find his owners.'

'Call me Kathleen, please.' The woman – Kathleen – didn't sound cross, at least. I edged a little closer to the packet with the smells in. 'He belongs to the family across the street, doesn't he?'

'The McCawleys,' Jack confirmed, and I felt my heart tighten at the word. They were just a name to Jack, and not even that to Kathleen. But to me, they were my world.

I missed them. I'd even consider giving up the interesting smells, just to have Jay here with me.

I reached out a paw to the paper wrapped around the smells. I said *consider*, after all. And it didn't look like Daisy, Oliver and the children were coming back any time soon.

Might as well make the most of my adventure while they were gone.

'He seems very interested in my gingerbread men,' Kathleen said. She reached over and plucked the paper from the table, just before I managed to knock it to the floor to explore its contents.

I gave a low growl of disappointment, and Kathleen chuckled. 'I wonder if this was what you came rushing in here for? Or perhaps it was the pot pourri in the hallway. That smells quite Christmassy, too.'

She took a plate from the dresser shelf, and lay it on the floor. Then, to my surprise – and Jack's, from the look on his face – she placed a piece of gingerbread onto it. It looked just like the pictures on the wrapping paper around the twins' Christmas present – right down to the sweetie buttons!

I risked a quick glance at Kathleen, then at Jack, then dived on it.

Gingerbread, for the record, is *glorious*.

'Well, he certainly seems to like that!' Jack said, laughing.

'Can I offer you some too? Or maybe a mince pie?' Kathleen asked. 'I'll even let you sit at the table to eat it. And make you a cup of tea to go with it, if you like?'

'I shouldn't ...' Jack started, but Kathleen had already fetched a second plate and put a mince pie and another gingerbread man on it. I'd tried mince pies last year, and been very sick. They were *nothing* compared to gingerbread.

'Please,' she said. 'My daughter has sent me this giant hamper of Christmas treats – puddings and biscuits and chocolates – but really, it can't make up for her not being here this Christmas. To be honest, I'd be grateful for someone to share it with. Please, stay.' She sounded almost desperate for the company, I thought. Obviously, Kathleen was looking for people to belong with – just like I was. And hadn't Jack said he wanted to find somewhere that could be home? Seemed to me, Kathleen's house with its gingerbread men was a pretty good start.

Jack must have thought so, too, because he sat down at the table, saying, 'Well, in that case ... Thank you.'

I had just wolfed down the rest of my gingerbread, when something occurred to me. Kathleen had said 'hamper'. Wasn't that the word Daisy had used to describe the box of interesting smells that morning? That had definitely had a lot more than just mince pies and gingerbread in it.

Which meant that, somewhere in the kitchen, there had to be all sorts of other interesting foods, waiting to be eaten. And maybe, if Jack and I stayed long enough, Kathleen would let me sample them, too …

DAISY

Getting the whole family back into the car and *off* the ferry in France wasn't any easier than it had been getting them on in the first place.

Bella had checked in with the Find Claude campaign just before they docked though, and while there wasn't much there yet, they had received one message from an older teenager who lived on Maple Drive, who said she'd seen Claude chasing a cat earlier in the day, before she saw the page.

'She's out shopping now,' Bella had reported, as she shut down the computer again. 'But she'll keep an eye out when she gets home.'

'At least we know he was okay this morning,' Daisy had said, sighing with relief. 'We'll just have to hope for another sighting soon.'

'Of course, this would be a lot easier to monitor if I had my phone ...'

But in all the chaos of getting off the ferry, Daisy still hadn't managed to find the key to the vanity case. And now they were safely in France, it seemed her parents hadn't even managed to make it out to meet them.

'Where did you arrange to meet them?' Oliver asked, surveying Caen's busy port.

'Well, we didn't. Not exactly,' Daisy admitted. She'd just assumed they'd be there, waiting to greet them. After all, it was their fault they'd come this far in the first place.

Oliver sighed. 'Do you have their French mobile numbers?'

'Only on my phone.' She remembered the receipt she'd found in her purse earlier. 'But I do have the number of the chateau.'

'Which we can't call, because we have no phones,' Bella pointed out. Again.

'Besides,' Oliver added, 'They're supposed to be *here*.'

But they weren't. Even Daisy could admit that, now the crowd was thinning out.

'There's a pay phone,' she said, spotting one across the way, and praying it took credit cards. Her head was pounding. Why couldn't anything just be simple for once? 'I'll give it a go. You stay here with the kids.'

'Daisy, darling!' Her mother's voice sounded the same as always; part distracted, part lovingly disappointed. 'Where *are* you? We expected you *hours* ago.'

Why? Daisy wondered. She'd given them the ferry times. She supposed they had written them down wrong. Or not written them down at all. Either was equally likely.

Once they'd got Jay's birthday wrong for three years in a row, thanks to a stubborn insistence that their calendar knew better than Daisy did when her own son was born.

'We've only just got the car off the ferry,' she said, knowing it wasn't worth arguing with her. Mum believed her own version of reality with a ferocity that defied all logic. 'I thought you were coming to meet us?'

'Well, it's just as well we didn't! Imagine how long we'd have had to wait.'

Right. Of course.

Daisy sighed, and rubbed her temples with her free hand. 'Look, we're here now. Can you give me some instructions on how to reach you?'

'Why not just use that fancy phone of Oliver's to find us?' Mum asked. 'He's always saying how it can do anything.'

Including playing mindless games and avoiding conversation with his family. 'We're having a technology-free Christmas,' Daisy informed her. That sounded much better than 'I accidentally locked all our phones and tablets in a case and lost the key.' Surely the key had to be somewhere. It would show up when she unpacked, Daisy was certain.

'I'll get your father,' Mum said, and dropped the phone before Daisy could object.

The last thing she wanted was her father's idea of helpful directions.

'Hello, my angel!' Dad sounded unnaturally jovial, so Daisy assumed gin and tonic hour had started a little earlier than normal this festive season. 'You made it to our fair country, then! Sorry we couldn't come and meet you. There was an issue with the range cooker your mother insisted on. Also, my latest nemesis – a collared dove who seems to think our kitchen is its new palace.'

'I thought she'd just written the time down wrong,' Daisy admitted, ignoring the part about the bird.

'Oh, she'd done that too. The calendar says you should have been here six hours ago.'

'The calendar is, once again, wrong.' Really, was it a surprise she was so unable to keep her own life in order? Look what she was descended from.

'It usually is.' There was a rustling noise at the other end, which Daisy knew from experience was her father organising his map collection. 'Now, you need directions, correct?'

'Yes. But Dad, just the simplest, most basic ones you can manage, please.'

'Of course!'

'Great.' Daisy pulled a leaky pen and an old receipt out of her bag and proceeded to take notes.

'Now, the thing you need to understand about French roads, is that there's always at least two ways of doing things. The way everyone else goes, and the best way. I'm going to tell you the best way.'

Oh God. Daisy rested her head against the plastic surround of the pay phone, and resigned herself to being lost for the next several hours.

Ten minutes later, with a series of scrawled instructions in hand, she hung up, and headed back towards her family.

'So?' Oliver asked, looking up from wiping what looked like apple mush from the twins' faces. 'Are they coming?'

Daisy shook her head. 'The calendar thought we should be here six hours ago, and there was some sort of trouble with the oven and a bird. Which hopefully won't affect dinner,' she added, as the thought occurred to her. Oliver and the kids would *not* be happy if she'd dragged them all this way, away from Claude, and there wasn't even a decent meal at the end of it.

'So what do we do now?' Bella asked. Jay was curled up in her lap, half asleep, apparently worn out by his epic crying fit earlier. His soft toy Claude was clasped tightly in his arms, black ears poking out, a poor substitute for the real thing.

'Grandad has given me directions,' Daisy said, and Oliver and Bella groaned in unison. 'I'm sure we'll be fine.'

Oliver tossed the apple-covered baby wipes into a nappy bag and stuck them in the side pocket of the change bag for

Daisy to deal with later. 'Well, if we want to get there before Christmas Day, we'd better set off now.'

'It's only an hour's drive, Dad says,' Daisy protested. 'And mostly on two or three roads. Depending on which way we go.'

Oliver paused. 'How many possible routes did he give you?'

'Well, he said there were two. And then he described six. Or seven. I might have lost count.'

Eyes raised to heaven, Oliver shouldered the change bag. 'Right.'

'It'll be fine.'

'You keep saying that,' Bella interjected.

'I keep hoping it's true,' Daisy said. 'It is the season of miracles, after all.'

But that logic was wearing thin, even for her.

Just one hour, and they'd be at the chateau. And then they could figure out how they were going to get home to Claude again.

JACK

'These mince pies are delicious. So is the gingerbread,' Jack said, watching as Claude devoured his third piece. Were dogs allowed to eat gingerbread? He suspected not, but he also knew he stood no chance of keeping Claude away from them. He just hoped the McCawleys didn't blame him for any ensuing stomach upset.

'I'm glad,' Kathleen said. 'I don't really have a sweet tooth, but I suspect my daughter sent them for me to give to guests. So they've served their purpose, I suppose!'

It seemed a shame that Jack and Claude were the only guests she had to share them with, but Jack couldn't help but feel grateful for the glimpse of the Maple Drive he'd been hoping for when he moved there.

'Your daughter won't be with you for Christmas?' He knew it could be difficult to get everyone together over the holidays, but he didn't like the thought of Kathleen alone this Christmas Day. And he couldn't help but think that if she were his mum, he'd make a point of being there. A hamper wasn't the same as company, after all.

Kathleen shook her head. 'Unfortunately not. She says she wants to be, of course, but … she lives in Australia, you see, and her husband's family are all over there …' She sighed. 'They're hoping to come over in the spring, instead, which will be nice. And perhaps my son will be able to join them – he's working over in America at the moment, on a five-year contract. But he's met a girl, so whether or not he comes back at all, we'll have to wait and see. All I know is that they're keeping him too busy to come home for Christmas!'

'You didn't think about going over there?' Kathleen was obviously disappointed to not have her family visiting, but then, America was a long way – and Australia even further.

'No, not really.' She gave him a half smile. 'It's probably just old age, or maybe I just did too much travelling in my younger days, but these days I just can't face getting on a plane. Lily and Hugh keep trying to persuade me to move out to Australia with them, where they can look after me. They go on and on about the quality of life, the opportunities, the weather ... but I lived abroad for so many years, now I really just want to spend my last days here, at home. Where I belong.'

'I know that feeling,' Jack admitted. 'But I'm sure you've got plenty of days left to enjoy your home!'

'I hope so! But not as many as you.' She studied him critically. 'So, you've spent time abroad too? Of course you have. Army?'

Jack nodded. 'Ten years. I saw a lot more of the world than I ever imagined existed when I was twenty-one.'

'I *would* say the same,' Kathleen said, with a grin. 'But I was married to a civil servant in the Foreign Office by the time I was nineteen. My whole world suddenly opened up, and I loved every moment of it.'

Jack thought about all the parcels he'd delivered to Kathleen over the last few months, each with exotic postmarks and interesting stamps, and often in unusual shapes and sizes. 'I did wonder. You get a lot more post from overseas than most people on my patch!'

'I still have a lot of friends, all over the world,' Kathleen said. 'Mostly we email, or Skype occasionally – it's amazing how easy it is to keep in touch these days. And many of them like to send packages at this time of year. I ship out a lot of tea and biscuits, myself!'

'I can imagine,' Jack said, with a laugh. 'But still, it's not the same as being with them, is it? Seeing the people you love, day after day, whenever you want.'

'No,' Kathleen admitted. 'It's not. So, how are you finding civilian life?'

'It's taken a little adjusting to,' Jack admitted. 'When you're in the forces, they take care of everything for you – I never had to worry about registering with a doctor before, or finding a place to rent or even buying my own socks! Everything I needed just showed up when I needed it, or I could just go down to stores and get it. Even my friends were just there, whenever I needed them.'

They sat in silence for a moment, sipping their tea, the only noise the sound of Claude wolfing down biscuits.

Then Kathleen said, 'You miss them, then? Your army family?'

How had she known? That they weren't just friends to him, they were family. The only family he'd known since his parents died.

'They *are* family, aren't they?' Kathleen went on, as if she'd read his mind. 'When you're together like that, strangers in a foreign land – and I imagine even training in this country you're that too. It must be nearly impossible for outsiders to understand the life you live, the challenges you face, the risks you take. So the people you serve with …'

'They become your brothers and sisters,' Jack admitted. 'And your parents, your children. Your people. It's been … hard. Leaving them behind.'

'I'm sure. Are you still in touch, though?'

Jack nodded. 'When we can be. We Skype occasionally. Email. Same as you, I suppose. But most of them, they have other people they want to talk to, when there's time. Their real family.'

'And you don't? No family on the outside?'

'Not any more.' Jack set down his empty teacup. How had he ended up opening up to this stranger? Were his secrets so cheaply bought, for a cup of tea and a mince pie?

Or maybe he'd just been waiting for somebody to tell them to. Someone who would understand.

He looked down at Claude, who was watching him from his seat on the floor. It sounded crazy, even in his head, but he couldn't shake the feeling that Claude had brought him into Kathleen's house for a reason. That he'd sensed that Kathleen needed the company – and maybe that Jack did, too.

Kathleen tilted her head as she looked at him. 'I have to ask … why did you leave? What were you looking for, back in the civilian world?'

And wasn't that just the question he'd been asking himself lately?

Jack fiddled with the silver case from his mince pie. 'Well …'

'I'm sorry,' Kathleen interrupted. 'You don't have to tell me. My daughter's always telling me I'm too nosy, asking all these questions.'

'No, it's okay,' Jack assured her. 'In fact … it's nice to have someone ask, to be honest.'

Kathleen smiled, with the same understanding she'd shown since he arrived. 'Well, in that case …'

'I guess it was just time. Ten years … that was a third of my life. And I loved it, I did. But I didn't want it to be the only thing I ever did. I wanted to have a life of my own as well, outside of the army. A place where I belonged. I just haven't quite found it yet.'

'And why is that, do you think?'

Jack considered. He'd been so sure he was looking in the wrong place, that Maple Drive couldn't give him what he wanted. But what he'd been looking for was a community, a place where he might be invited in for a cup of tea and a chat, where he would know everyone's names. And yes, maybe a place where he might find love, family, and a future that he was excited to wake up to every morning. But those things took time, like Bill said. And right now…

Well, there he was, drinking tea and having that chat – thanks to Claude, anyway. And he *did* know all his neighbours names, even if they didn't know his yet. But maybe that was because he hadn't told them. Hadn't said, 'Hi, I'm Jack. I'm your new postman – and I live around the corner, by the way.'

Yes, the inhabitants of Maple Drive might not all make much of an effort to get to know each other. But in the last twelve hours he'd had long, proper conversations with most of them – starting with Mrs Templeton and her aversion to icicle lights, then Holly and her cat lead, all the neighbours who didn't know Claude, and now Kathleen.

Not bad for one day. And he hadn't even been trying.

Imagine how he might get on if he made an actual effort.

'I think,' he said, realising that Kathleen was still waiting for an answer to her question. 'I think I was waiting for it to come to me, rather than going out and looking for it. But I think I'm ready for that to change, too.'

Kathleen beamed. 'Well, that is good news! So, tell me about this life you're looking for then. When you get to my age, other people's dreams and ambitions are the only things you can look forward to!'

It was the second time she'd said something like that, like there was nothing left to her life except waiting for the end. And yes, okay, she wasn't young any more, Jack could see that. But still, he didn't like the idea of Kathleen counting down to her death.

Suddenly, he wanted to give her something to look forward to. Something to remind her that there were still good things in the world for her.

But how on earth would he, Jack Tyler, go about that? He had no idea.

So instead, he settled back to tell her about his hopes for his new, civilian life.

'I guess I was looking for somewhere to belong, more than anything.' As he spoke, he felt a furry head press against his leg, and reached down to rub Claude between the ears. The little dog apparently took that as permission to jump up into his lap.

Kathleen smiled at the sight. 'Looks to me like you belong to somebody already.'

Jack shook his head. 'This little fella is only on loan,' he explained. 'As soon as the McCawleys get home, he's going back.'

'Perhaps,' Kathleen replied. 'But I think you've made an impact on him already. And once a dog is attached to someone … he won't forget you anyway, is my bet.'

'That's a nice thought,' Jack admitted. He quite liked the

idea of Claude popping out to say hello whenever he had post for number 11. He looked down at the small dog in his lap. His ears were lowered, and Jack suspected his eyes were closed. Every now and again his rear end wiggled, as if he were wagging his stumpy tail. 'In the meantime, I'd better go and see if I can find him a home for the night. I'm not allowed pets at my rental,' he explained.

Kathleen looked concerned. 'Any ideas? I'd take him myself, but I'm a little too old to learn how to care for a dog!'

'You're never too old,' Jack said. 'But don't worry. I'm going to take him next door to Holly, first, and return her lead. I'm sure the McCawleys will be back by then.' As long as they hadn't gone away. But if they had … surely they'd have realised Claude was missing and come back for him by now? Or made arrangements for someone to take care of him?

'Holly, is it?' Kathleen asked, with a knowing smile. 'She seems like a sweet girl, not that we've talked much.'

'Claude broke into her house earlier, too,' Jack explained. 'Through the cat flap.'

Kathleen laughed. 'I'd like to have seen that!'

'He basically did a belly flop,' Jack said, smiling at the memory. Then he rubbed Claude's back to try and wake him. 'Come on, Claude. Time to get up.'

Sleepily, Claude opened one eye, and stared at Jack. With a bit of prodding, he jumped down to the floor and Jack reattached the lead. They might only be walking next door, but Jack wasn't taking any chances.

'Are you sure you can't stay a little longer?' Kathleen's eyes were sad as she reached out to grab Jack's hand. 'I get so few actual visitors these days … and I've so enjoyed our chat.'

'So have I,' Jack assured her, feeling a little guilty about leaving. She looked so lonely … 'But I'm afraid I really do have to go. Maybe I could come back, though? Another day?'

Kathleen's face brightened, and she squeezed his hand before letting go. 'I'd like that a lot.'

'Then it's a plan.' Jack tugged Claude away from where he was optimistically sniffing around at the bottom of the counter where Kathleen's hamper sat. 'Come on, boy. Time to go and see Holly.'

Claude trotted obediently back towards the front door at the sound of Holly's name, and Jack followed. He was starting to think that Claude understood a lot more than Jack had given him credit for.

'Thanks again for the tea and mince pies,' Jack said, stepping outside. Beside him, Claude shivered in the cold. 'And Claude's gingerbread. I hope you have a lovely Christmas, if I don't make it back before then.'

'And I hope you find everything that you're looking for,' Kathleen told him, pressing a last piece of gingerbread into his hand. Claude barked his approval at that.

'So do I,' Jack admitted. But he knew a pretty good place to start – with a visit to Holly. 'Merry Christmas,' he called, before heading next door, whistling 'Jingle Bells' as he walked, Claude trotting alongside him, waiting for his gingerbread.

CHAPTER
SIX

CLAUDE

Sleepily, I kept pace with Jack, as his long legs covered the short distance between Kathleen's and Holly's houses in big strides. Glancing across the road, I saw that there was still no car in the driveway of my home, and no lights on either. Still no McCawleys.

I sighed. It was a shame, really. I could quite happily have stayed napping at Kathleen's house until Daisy and Oliver found their way home for me – especially if she kept feeding me such delicious gingerbread. But Jack obviously had his own reasons for wanting to go back to Holly's house. I had my suspicions about what they were, too.

Obviously, humans weren't all that different from us animals. We both wanted to find our people, our pack. To belong, to have somewhere to call home – whether that was a whole house or a basket with a blanket. For me, my people were very clear in my mind, I knew exactly where I belonged – even if they seemed to have forgotten.

But Jack didn't seem to know where *his* home was at all, or which people he belonged to.

Maybe he could belong to Holly, or to Kathleen. Kathleen had the advantage of no Perdita and gingerbread, but Holly … Jack had seemed very happy when we were there earlier.

I resolved to watch more closely this time, to see how he acted around her. Whether she might be home for Jack – and if so, how I could help him realise it. Sometimes people needed a little push, I'd found – like a cold nose in the ear when Oliver slept in past my breakfast time, or a bit of nuzzling to persuade Jay to put down his tablet and pet me.

I liked Jack. I liked the idea of him finding home, and finding it somewhere that meant he was on hand to rub between my ears whenever I needed it.

After all, the McCawleys *had* left me behind. It was only natural that I'd have to find some new people to help fill the gulf that stretched between us now. At least until they came back.

Jack knocked on Holly's door, and I sat patiently beside him on the mat, sparkly lead attached. There was no need to escape this time; I felt certain that Holly would let me in. She'd seemed quite taken with me that morning, *and* she'd given me some of Perdita's food.

It had been okay, I supposed. But maybe she'd been shopping for actual dog food while Jack and I were off working.

Yes, that seemed about right. Really, I'd fallen on my paws. Abandoned, left behind in the freezing winter, and I'd managed to find *three* people who wanted to feed and look after me.

It was all down to natural charm.

Holly opened the door, a bright smile on her face, and then looked down at me. 'No luck finding the McCawleys then?'

'Afraid not,' Jack said, reaching down to pat my back. It wasn't as good as a rub between the ears, but it *was* comforting. 'You took your icicles down?'

Icicles? I sat back and looked up at the house. It did seem darker, I supposed.

Holly's cheeks were red. 'Don't worry. They're going back

up tomorrow. And then some.'

'So you took them down because …?'

'I had a run-in with Mrs Templeton,' Holly explained. I butted up against her leg in sympathy.

I'd had run-ins with Mrs Templeton before. I wouldn't even wish them on *Perdita*.

'You'd better come in,' Holly said, standing aside to let Jack and me past. 'Before she comes out to complain about loitering postmen too. Although heaven knows what she'll think we're up to in here.'

Jack laughed. 'I'm sure she doesn't care what you do in the privacy of your own home. She just has a bit of a thing about the appearance of the street, I think.'

Holly and I both gave him sceptical looks. 'I bet she's watching,' Holly said. 'Right now.'

We all peered out into the darkness, towards the drawn curtains of number 13 Maple Drive. As we watched, one of the curtains on the ground floor suddenly twitched and lay flat again.

'See!' Holly crowed, triumphantly. 'She is the original curtain-twitching neighbour! Quick, get inside before we give her anything more to talk about.'

Jack laughed. 'You seem very jolly for someone who is being spied on by her next door neighbour.'

'I had to test the mulled wine.' Holly headed into the kitchen. Jack dropped my lead as soon as the front door closed, so I trotted after her, hoping there might be some more gingerbread in my future. Or at least some cat food. 'Would you like some?' she called back over her shoulder.

'That would be great, thanks,' Jack said. 'I am officially off duty now until the day after Boxing Day, so I feel like I should celebrate.'

'You absolutely should.' She handed him a glass full of dark red liquid. I sat at her feet and looked up hopefully. She sighed as she spotted me. 'I suppose you're hungry again, aren't you? Well, you won't like mulled wine, Claude, I can tell you that much.'

'I wouldn't be so sure. He's a huge fan of gingerbread – not that I recommend giving him any more,' Jack said. 'He just ate three gingerbread men next door. He's probably going to be sick later.'

Clearly, these humans did not understand the power of my stomach. I widened my eyes, and gave a small whimper to encourage Holly to give up the goods.

'No more gingerbread,' she said, firmly. 'I haven't even got around to decorating my gingerbread house yet. But you can have some more of Perdita's food, if you're really hungry.'

I followed her to the cupboard with Perdita's things in, past a table holding a whole miniature *house* made of gingerbread. Maybe, if I was really nice to Holly, she'd let me have some, eventually. But in the meantime, cat food it was. It wasn't ideal, but at least it had an added advantage of annoying my nemesis. That counted for a lot.

'What about you?' I heard her ask Jack, as I tucked into the cat food. 'Are you full of gingerbread, too?'

'A bit,' Jack admitted. 'But actually, our visit next door gave me an idea. Something I'd like to talk to you about.'

'Really? That sounds interesting,' Holly said.

I zoned out and focused on the bowl in front of me. I figured if they were talking about food I could always start listening in again. In the meantime, I had more important things to think about.

Like how to get to that gingerbread house. And how to convince Jack to stay in Maple Drive.

DAISY

'Okay. Everyone stand back.' Daisy lifted the umbrella over her head and prepared to smash the lock of the vanity case.

This had officially gone on long enough. Not only were they down one dog, they'd been lost in the wilds of northern France for the past hour and a half without even a phone to call for help. It was already the worst Christmas on record, and they hadn't even made it to Christmas Eve yet.

It was time to take serious action.

'Wait!' Oliver cried, but she ignored him, slamming the handle of the umbrella against the tiny metal lock.

Nothing happened.

'Yeah, I could have told you that wasn't going to work,' Oliver said, and Daisy felt the anger and frustration rising through her body at his words.

'That's so incredibly helpful,' she ground out, between her clenched teeth. 'And I suppose you have the answers to all our problems, right? I suppose you can get us back home through some sort of teleportation device, saving Claude from being alone on Christmas Eve, and us from having to spend Christmas in my parents' crumbling chateau?' Jay wailed in the back seat at the reminder of Claude, and Daisy's jaw tightened painfully at the noise.

Why was everything she planned always such a *disaster*?

'I just wanted to say that there has to be a better way to get into that case,' Oliver snapped back. 'And if you hadn't locked my phone in there in the first place—'

'Because *of course* this is all *my* fault,' Daisy interrupted, even though she had a sneaking suspicion it might be.

'If *you* hadn't locked the phones in there at least we'd have the sat nav and we wouldn't be lost in the middle of sodding France!' Oliver finished.

'Language!' Daisy yelled, as the twins began to cry again.

'Oh for God's sake.' Bella clambered forward, between the twins' car seats and grabbed the vanity case. 'Let me have a go.' She pulled a hair grip from her messy bun and jammed it into the lock, twisting it round a few times until the lid popped open.

Daisy and Oliver stared.

'Do I want to know where you learned how to do that?' Daisy asked, pretty sure she didn't.

Bella shrugged. 'YouTube.'

'Right.'

Grabbing her phone from the pile, and tossing Jay his tablet, Bella clambered back. 'Okay, we've got a message on the Find Claude page.'

Daisy's heart jumped. Had someone found him? Was he safe and warm inside somewhere cosy and welcoming? 'And?'

'Hang on …' Bella's fingers swiped across the screen as she accessed the message. 'Okay, it's from the same girl – Jessica, at number 3. She's back from shopping and watching out, but no sign of Claude yet.' Daisy's heart sank back down to its usual position. 'Oh, this is good – she's shared the page with all her friends, and they're sharing it too. *Someone* will spot him soon, for sure.' She spoke the last to Jay, who snuggled against her side in response.

'I hope so,' Daisy murmured. Poor Claude.

Bella wrapped one arm around Jay, and kept the other on her phone. 'Hey, want me to check if there's anywhere to eat around here? I'm starving.'

'That would be … remarkably helpful,' Daisy admitted. They all needed something to eat.

Oliver, meanwhile, had retrieved his phone and gone back to sulking in the passenger seat. With a sigh, Daisy picked hers up too. Three missed calls – all from Mum, earlier in the day, before she'd phoned her from Caen. Nothing from anyone else – certainly nobody who might know where Claude was.

She was going to have to call Mrs Templeton, that much was clear. Even if Bella's Find Claude campaign worked, it was irresponsible not to use every possible avenue to get Claude somewhere safe. But maybe it could wait until after they'd all had something to eat. Claude would understand that, Daisy was sure. The dog did always think with his stomach, after all.

'Okay, it looks like we're about ten miles off the main road we're *supposed* to be on,' Oliver said, swiping along the map on his phone.

'There's a McDonald's about a mile away, or a small town that might have restaurants a bit further along,' Bella added.

Jay, meanwhile, had started up the lullaby app on his tablet, which had finally persuaded the twins to stop screaming.

Daisy tried to ignore how much easier her life had just become with the addition of technology, and focused on the important things.

'Town,' she decided. 'I want a proper meal, in a proper

restaurant. And I am going to have a very large glass of wine with it.' Oliver raised his eyebrows, and she added, 'Because *you* are driving the rest of the way. I am done.'

Sensibly, Oliver chose not to argue.

HOLLY

Maybe it was the mulled wine and the Christmas music playing softly in the background that made Jack look even more attractive in the subdued under-cabinet lighting of her kitchen, but Holly doubted it. She had a feeling he'd always been this good looking and she just hadn't let herself notice it.

Or maybe it was just that any man who was as passionate and engaged in his Christmas planning couldn't help but look gorgeous. Especially when he was doing a good deed.

'So, she's all alone for Christmas too?' Holly asked, as Jack finished his summary of his and Claude's visit next door. Holly had exchanged the odd hello or how are you with Kathleen since she moved in, but that was about all. The older woman usually seemed to be busy bustling about on errands or catching the bus somewhere on the weekends, and Holly was usually rushing to get to work during the week, so their paths rarely crossed for more than a few moments every morning. Plus there was always the fear that Kathleen Nordmann might be another curtain twitcher like Mrs Templeton.

But from Jack's description, Kathleen sounded far more like someone Holly should get to know. And if she wasn't mistaken, Jack's idea was going to involve her doing just that.

'Yeah. Her daughter and son can't make it over, and I think

all her other friends are miles away. I guess she's a bit lonely, to be honest, from the way she welcomed Claude and me in.' He tilted his head slightly, obviously remembering the experience. 'More than a bit, in fact. She wanted us to stay. As it is, I promised I'd go back soon because she's very, very alone.'

'It does sound like it.' Guilt gnawed at Holly's insides. Had she been so wrapped up in her own dramas that she'd totally failed to notice that the woman next door – the one she saw almost every day – needed a friend? Maybe even as much as Holly did. Jack had noticed, though, and he was planning to do something about it. The least she could do was help.

'Anyway, I just thought that maybe, if you had the time, we could do something for her? To brighten up her Christmas?' Jack phrased it as a question, but to Holly it was already a definite plan. They needed to do this.

And if it gave her an excuse to spend rather more time in the company of the cute postman than she normally would, well, that could only be a Christmas bonus, right?

'Like a surprise? We absolutely should,' she said, firmly. 'What were you thinking of?'

Jack pulled a face and shrugged. 'To be honest, that's pretty much as far as I'd got. I figured you might have some ideas?' He waved a hand over her parade of Christmas crafts. 'I mean, you seem to have this Christmas thing pretty much nailed.'

Holly felt an emptiness opening up inside her chest, one that she'd been avoiding all day. 'Christmas *is* my favourite time of the year,' she admitted.

'I kind of got that.' Jack gave her a fond smile, not unlike the one he'd given Claude when the little dog had dozed off right next to Perdita's food bowl a few moments ago. Holly bristled a little inside. She didn't want him to see her as a cute, fluffy thing. But then, she'd not really given him any reason to see anything more, had she?

Maybe she needed to work on that.

'I'm sorry,' Jack said. 'You've probably got loads of Christmas plans already, and no time to help me out with this, and you're just too polite to say.' He raised his glass of mulled wine to his lips and took a big gulp. 'I should get out of your way.'

'No!' Holly said, loud enough to make Claude stir in his sleep. 'No, really,' she went on, a little quieter, her hand on his arm for emphasis. 'I'm glad you suggested it. It sounds like a really kind, thoughtful idea, and I'd love to be involved.'

'Really?' Jack looked down at her hand, and Holly resisted the urge to pull it away in embarrassment. If she wanted him to see her as more than a sweet crafty girl on his post round, she needed to show him that she was more. 'You're not going away for Christmas or anything?'

Holly winced at that, and sat back. 'No. Not any more.'

'But, you *had* plans?' Jack guessed. 'Sorry. You don't have to tell me if you don't want to.'

'It's okay.' Holly shook her head. 'Actually … tomorrow was supposed to be my wedding day.'

Jack's expression settled into the pitying look she'd elicited from everyone she'd seen for weeks after Sebastian left. Every time she'd had to tell a friend or family member or colleague that the wedding was off, every time anyone mentioned weddings or romance or love, or even bloody Christmas, she'd got that look. That *poor little Holly, all alone and abandoned. However will she cope?* look.

Basically, the look she'd given Claude that morning when she realised he was alone too.

God, she was as pathetic as a lost French Bulldog with

ridiculous ears. What did that say about her life?

'Honestly, I'm better off without him,' she said, firmly. *She* believed it. She just wished other people would too.

'So you called it off?' Jack asked.

'Well … no. Not exactly,' she admitted. 'But it's been a few months and I can honestly say I'm glad he left.'

'That's good.' Jack nodded, uncomfortably. Holly got the impression this wasn't exactly the conversation he'd been planning on having with her, and he had no idea where to go with it next.

She knew she should drop it. She'd given him more than enough information on the subject, and the last thing he probably wanted was her bemoaning her past relationships. But somehow, the words kept tumbling out anyway.

'The thing is, it turned out he just wanted to marry me as a way to get a promotion. But then he got this new job in Dubai and didn't need me any more.'

Jack's expression changed at that, moving from pity towards something like … was it *anger*? Holly wasn't sure.

'That utter bastard,' he said, each word hard and fierce.

'Yes,' Holly agreed. 'He is. So, like I say, much better off now. I mean, he didn't even like Christmas.'

It took a second, but Jack's face lightened at that, and he laughed. 'Really? How on earth did you two even get together? And who doesn't like Christmas, anyway?'

'Exactly what I said.' Holly motioned to her pile of crafts. 'I mean, what's not to like?'

'Well, that depends. Did you make him carry the air drying clay?'

Holly giggled, and slapped him lightly on the wrist. 'No, I didn't. I don't think he had the muscles, anyway.'

Jack raised his eyebrows slightly, and Holly's eyes widened. Oh God, she'd just pointed out that she'd noticed his muscles! Well, she had wanted to make it obvious that she was interested ...

'What about your family?' Jack asked. 'Are you not spending Christmas with them?'

Holly sighed. Back to the subject of her festive misery. 'Normally I'd be visiting my parents,' she explained. 'But this year ... well, they'd saved all this money for my wedding, and then all of a sudden they didn't need it. The wedding cancellation insurance paid out pretty quickly, and they decided to spend it on a Christmas cruise.'

'Leaving you here on your own.'

'I told them I'd be spending Christmas with friends,' Holly admitted. 'They deserved the holiday. They've been brilliant this year, what with everything.'

'So why *aren't* you spending it with friends?' Jack asked.

Because I don't have any. All my friends were Sebastian's friends first. It wasn't quite the truth – she also had old university friends she hadn't seen in years who lived miles away or colleagues locally with families of their own, but no one she felt she could call up and confess the depths of her loneliness to. No one whose Christmas she'd feel comfortable gate-crashing. So instead she said, 'Well, I'm hoping I will be. If we can work together to come up with something for Kathleen.' Jack smiled at that, and Holly knew she was on the right track. But it did lead her to another question. She frowned. 'But what about you? Don't you have Christmas plans?'

Jack shook his head, shifting in his chair so he was leaning away from her again. She hadn't even realised they'd leaned in, but as she sat up straighter too she realised they must have been pretty close. 'Not this year,' he said, shortly.

Well, if he thought he was getting away with that as an answer, he had another thing coming. Holly had just poured out all the misery of the past four months to him. The least he could offer was a proper full sentence of explanation.

'No family?' she pressed. 'Friends?'

'My parents died when I was twenty-one,' he said, and Holly winced.

'I'm so sorry. I didn't know.'

He shrugged. 'No reason you should. And my friends … they're all still in the army. Kind of hard to have a Christmas get-together when most of you are on manoeuvres.'

'The army?' Well, that explained a lot. Like the muscles. 'You were a soldier?'

'Until earlier this year,' Jack confirmed. 'And now I'm a postman.'

'And is that better or worse?' She couldn't imagine being in the army, miles away from home a lot of the time, never knowing where you might be sent next. She liked her home – her little house, her cat, her craft space.

'It's different,' Jack said. 'Lonelier, in a way, which is odd. I mean, I see hundreds of people every day, but …'

'It's not the same as having people to talk to,' Holly finished for him. 'I know what you mean. I mean, I'm a teacher, and I talk to kids all day, encouraging them to think about their dreams, their plans for the future. And I talk with their parents about their hopes for their kids. But there's no one to ask about my dreams, or my hopes.' Just once, it would be nice to have someone who wanted to know what her dreams were. Where she wanted to go in her life, rather than how far she could get their kids.

'Exactly,' Jack said. 'At least, until today.'

Holly looked up and found his gaze on her, their eyes locking as she thought about everything that had changed since that morning, when he knocked on her door with Claude at his side. 'Yes,' she murmured. 'Until today.'

How could his eyes be so dark and deep? And how come she never noticed before? How could she ever have just dismissed him as 'the cute postman'?

Suddenly, he was all she could see.

And that sort of focus was dangerous. Hadn't she learnt that lesson by now? She'd looked at Sebastian the same way once, thought he was everything she wanted, focused so deeply on the parts that she loved that she hadn't even *noticed* or let herself acknowledge the parts that were less than perfect. Quite a long way than perfect, as it turned out.

A flirtation, a bit of fun, was one thing. But the moment she started obsessing about Jack's eyes … that signalled trouble.

'So, we're all alone this Christmas,' Holly said, pulling back. 'You, me and Kathleen, I mean.'

'And Claude,' Jack added. There was a hint of confusion in his eyes, but Holly ignored it.

'Of course. And Claude.' She glanced down at the little dog, still snoozing by Perdita's bowl. 'So, what are we going to do about that?'

'Well, for Kathleen … I thought maybe you might have some ideas?' Jack said hopefully.

Holly grinned. 'As it happens, I do. I think we should definitely keep it a surprise until the day, for a start. I'm thinking festive food, maybe some music … and definitely decorations! I just placed an order for some more lights to be delivered tomorrow. And there's going to be way more than I can fit on my house!' Just imagining Mrs Templeton's face when she saw numbers 12 and 10 Maple Drive lit up like Christmas trees gave Holly a glowing, happy feeling.

'Perfect!'

'What about the rest, though?' Holly considered, and answered her own question. 'Like, what food? A Christmas mini-feast? I've got some stuff here, but we could pick up a load of canapés and stuff to share? It might be easier than doing a whole Christmas dinner for the three of us, and that way if Kathleen isn't keen she can just have a few nibbles and go.'

'You're right,' Jack agreed. 'I'm no chef, and it's not like the three of us know each other very well. Spending the whole of Christmas together might be asking a bit much.'

'Exactly.' Holly tried to stamp down the feeling of disappointment that rose up at his words. Of course they weren't all going to spend Christmas together. Before today, they'd barely spoken three words between them. This was just a kind gesture to a lonely old lady, then they could all get back to their regular, scheduled lives.

Easy as pie. Or Christmas pudding, in this case.

'Great. Well, maybe we can get together again tomorrow to figure out exactly what we want to do?' Jack suggested. 'I can go shopping for food and things, if you like?'

'We'll come up with a shopping list,' Holly agreed.

'Which only leaves us with one question.' Holly followed Jack's gaze, and realised exactly what he meant.

'What do we do with Claude?' she said.

CHAPTER
SEVEN

CLAUDE

As a family pet, I've discovered it's always a good idea to keep one ear open for my name. Sometimes, it's followed by 'it's time for dinner' which isn't something I ever want to miss. More often, it's a 'Where is that dog? Did you see what he did to my shoes?' sort of call, at which point it's always a good idea to make a run for it. Or, more usually, hide under the bed. Occasionally, it precedes the words 'it's time to go to the vet's,' and then I really *do* run.

This time, the voices were different, and the conversation they were having about me even more disturbing than the suggestion of the vet and his needles.

'What do we do about Claude?' Holly said, and sighed, which was my first sign that there was something wrong.

I'd thought it was pretty obvious. I was going to go home with Jack, via a shop that sold dog food, and spend my evening having my ears scratched and my tummy rubbed. Easy.

Except that didn't seem to be what Jack and Holly were thinking.

'I was reading up, while you were gone,' Holly said. 'About what to do with lost dogs, I mean. The council website says you have to report any found dogs to them, even if you know who they belong to, if you can't find their owners.'

'Really?' Jack asked. 'I wonder why that is.'

I risked opening one eye in time to see Holly shrug. 'I think it's in case there's any dispute later – like the McCawleys could accuse us of trying to steal their dog.'

'But they left him here!' Jack pointed out. 'They've been gone all day, and there's no sign of them coming back yet. Poor Claude has been stuck out in the cold the whole time.'

'I know,' Holly said, sympathetically. I shut my eyes again as she looked down at me. No point letting on I was listening in until I knew what they'd decided. 'But we still have to call.'

Jack sighed. 'Okay. But then what? I can't take him home with me – my landlord doesn't allow pets.'

I gave a low growl in my supposed sleep. What kind of an idiot doesn't allow pets?

'And he can't stay here. Perdita's asleep upstairs. She'll lose it if she comes down and finds him here in the night.' Holly sounded genuinely sorry about the situation, but that didn't change the fact that I was still homeless. 'Wasn't there any-body in the street that had their mobile numbers or anything?'

'Nobody,' Jack replied, sounding glum. He obviously remembered all the hurtful ear comments, too. 'This estate isn't nearly as friendly as it looks from the outside.'

'I suppose not,' Holly said. 'When I moved here, I thought it would be a proper community, you know? With street par-ties and people popping by with cake and stuff.'

Jack smiled. 'Me too. That's why I picked it. But as it is … I can't see me staying much longer, to be honest.' I risked peeping again, wanting to see Holly's reaction.

'Really?' Holly went very still, but I don't think Jack noticed. Silly man.

'Yeah. I've already applied for a transfer, actually.'

'Right.' She sounded disappointed. 'Well. That's a shame. What if the next postman can't carry all my craft supplies?' She gave a little smile after that, but I didn't believe it was real. She thought Jack leaving was as bad an idea as I did.

'I'm sure he'll cope,' Jack said, but he looked a little sad at the idea, too.

'And Claude will miss you,' Holly added, and my ears twitched at the sound of my name. 'What *are* we going to do with him?'

'Call the council, I suppose,' Jack said, with a sigh. 'See what they say. If the McCawleys don't make it back tonight, and neither of us can keep him overnight … there's probably a shelter they'll take him to until his owners can collect him.'

Holly's nose scrunched up at that. 'The pound?'

Wait. What? I gave up the pretence of being asleep and sat up, looking between them, waiting for them to laugh. This had to be a joke, right? No way would Holly and Jack send me to the pound. No way. Not when I'd spent my whole day trying to find Jack a home, and Kathleen and Holly people to stop them being lonely. They wouldn't do that to me.

'Do you have the number at the council?' Jack asked. 'We'd better call before it gets any later. Who knows if they'll be open tomorrow with it being Christmas Eve.'

'I wrote it down. Hang on.' Holly disappeared into the hall, and Jack stared after her. They were really doing this.

Even if I found a place for Jack in Maple Drive, it looked like there wasn't one for me. With the McCawleys gone, I didn't belong anywhere at all.

What on earth was I going to do? My little heart beat double time just at the idea of being sent away, of not being here when Daisy and Oliver came back.

Of not being wanted at all.

I had a few moments while Holly found the phone number, I realised. Just a few moments to decide what happened next in my life.

Did I wait here, as if I were still tethered by that sparkly pink lead, and wait for them to send me off to the pound? The place where the abandoned dogs went to die?

Or did I take my life in my own hands, and find my own future – and maybe even my family?

Put like that, it was no competition.

With one last mouthful of Perdita's dinner, I checked Jack wasn't watching, and made a dash for the cat flap. It was an even tighter squeeze than it had been getting in that morning – probably due to the gingerbread – but I made it. As it swung shut behind me I heard Jack calling my name, but it was too late.

Shivering a little in the cold, winter air, I trotted off through the bushes, ducking through into the next garden before Jack could get the back door unlocked and come out looking for me.

I couldn't trust him, or Holly, any more. They might find their own people, but they *definitely* weren't mine.

I was on my own now.

And I had no idea what to do next.

DAISY

'Well, this is it.' Daisy stared up at the improbable building her parents had decided to call home. It had battlements. Honest to God battlements. 'You know, when they said chateau, I didn't think they meant something quite so literal in translation.'

Maybe it was the wine with dinner, but Daisy was finding it hard to be too alarmed at the crumbling castle her parents had apparently bought. At this point in the day's trials and tribulations, as long as it had hot running water and wine in the fridge, she was happy.

Then something dark and furry swooped overhead, past the windscreen, and for a moment Daisy considered just asking Oliver to turn the car around. They could sleep in the ferry terminal, right?

'It's cool,' Jay said, eyes wide, as he hugged his Claude substitute close.

'It's weird,' Bella countered with a frown, as another something swooped overhead. Really. Bats. Just what this Christmas needed to be perfect.

Daisy tried not to think about how much she hated bats.

The twins, finally both asleep in their car seats, had nothing to add. Oliver, from the driver's seat, looked too traumatised by driving on the right hand side of the road to comment.

Daisy unbuckled her seatbelt. 'Well, come on then. Let's go and see Granny and Grandad.' At least there wouldn't be any bats *inside* the chateau.

Probably.

Her parents were waiting for them at the door, faces lit by the lantern lights they'd hung above the doorway, all wide smiles and open arms. Daisy let herself be enfolded into a welcoming hug, and wondered exactly how she was going to break it to them that they had to leave again in the morning, ferries depending.

'Where's Claude?' her mum asked, peering into the darkness. 'You haven't left him in the car, poor creature! Petal is desperate to see him. Jerry, get Claude out of the boot.'

'Wait, Dad,' Daisy said, as her dad hurried to obey. 'Claude ... Claude's not actually with us.'

Mum's mouth dropped into a narrow O shape, her eyes wide and worried. 'He's not ... something didn't happen on the ferry, did it? I knew it was a bad idea, bringing a dog over here on the ferry! You know how they like to jump into the water! Oh, Jerry, didn't I say?'

'No,' Dad said, succinctly. 'You didn't. And neither did Daisy. What happened, love?'

'The stupid dog jumped out of the car before we even left Maple Drive,' Oliver explained. 'Jay had put his soft toy in the cage too, so we didn't even realise until we got on the ferry in Portsmouth and opened the boot.'

'So Claude's ... alive?' Mum asked. Daisy tried not to roll her eyes at the dramatics. Then she spotted Jay's lower lip quivering, and jumped in to reassure him.

'Of course he is! He's just fine, living it up at home. Probably hasn't even noticed we're not there!' She wrapped an arm around Jay's shoulders as she spoke in her jolliest voice, and hoped to God there was more wine in her future. 'But it does mean we're going to have to get back to him as soon as we can. There were no more ferries today because of the weather, but we're on standby for the one first thing tomorrow morning.'

'But tomorrow is Christmas Eve!' Mum cried.

I know, Mother. That's why we're here, remember?

Daisy sighed, and tried to keep her composure. 'I know, it's a real shame. But we have brought the M&S hamper, at least!'

Her mother perked up at the prospect of proper smoked salmon and Christmas pud, so Daisy ushered them all out of the hallway, past a lopsided Christmas tree with red and gold baubles, and into the house proper, lugging Luca in his car seat. Oliver deposited Lara's on the dusty stone floor and went back for the cases.

'Granny? What's your WiFi password?' Bella asked, as she headed into the lounge, phone in hand.

'WiFi?' Mum asked. 'Oh, Bell, we've barely got the phone line set up yet! It's been *such* a palaver.'

Bella stopped walking abruptly. 'So there's no internet *at all*?'

'Not in the house, love, no. Can't get much of a phone signal down here, either, although sometimes I can pick one up in the bedrooms.'

'I'll have to use roaming on my phone, then,' Bella said, obviously bracing herself for objections from her parents. Daisy elbowed Oliver as he groaned.

'Of course you can, love,' Daisy said. 'Especially if it's for Claude.'

Bella rolled her eyes, but headed off to try and find a signal.

'Ready for a glass, Daisy?' Dad asked, and she nodded. Enthusiastically.

JACK

Searching for a black and white furred dog in the dark of a winter evening was not easy, Jack was finding. Every flash of movement drew his eye, but more often than not it was another cat, or just the wind in the trees, or once, a startled looking fox.

'Claude!' Jack called again, but there was no sign of the absurd creature.

Sighing, Jack sank down to sit on the bus shelter bench again. How had his day reached this point? All he'd wanted to do was flirt innocently with the pretty blonde at number 12. Now they were spending Christmas together – along with her elderly neighbour – and he was spending his free evening searching for a dog that wasn't even his.

He blamed Claude for everything. If he hadn't broken into Holly's through the cat flap, or escaped into Kathleen's house in search of gingerbread … if he just hadn't run away.

Why had he run? Jack knew that dogs could be intelligent creatures, but it seemed a bit farfetched to imagine that he'd heard them talk about calling the pound and actually understood what that meant. More likely, he'd heard Perdita coming downstairs, or smelled something more interesting to eat than cat food outside and gone off in search of it.

The little dog seemed incapable of acting independently from the whims of his stomach.

Jack's own stomach growled, and he realised it had been quite a while since Kathleen's mince pies. He needed to go home, eat dinner and get ready for the next day. But how could he, knowing that Claude was still out there somewhere?

Number 11, the McCawleys' house, remained in darkness, although Jack had tried hammering on the door a few times just in case. The car was still missing, too. More and more it looked like they had gone away for Christmas – but Jack couldn't understand why they wouldn't have made suitable arrangements for Claude before they left. Mrs McCawley had seemed a little, well, scatty when he'd delivered parcels there before, but she certainly hadn't seemed cruel.

He couldn't help but think something must have gone very wrong, somewhere.

And how was he going to explain to them that he'd lost their dog, just after rescuing him? He'd put a note through their door on his rounds earlier, explaining the situation and leaving his phone number, just in case they returned while he was delivering mail to another street. So they'd know exactly who to come to when Claude wasn't there when they got home.

What would he tell them? And what would he tell Holly? She'd seemed distraught at the idea of Claude out there alone in the night, too.

If only he hadn't run for it. Jack was sure he'd have been able to come up with something, even if it meant smuggling the little dog into his house for the night and hoping his landlord never found out. It wasn't like he'd actually have let Claude go to the pound anyway. As soon as Holly had said it he'd known it wasn't an option. He'd have called the council, if that was the rule. But he wouldn't have let anyone take Claude away from Maple Drive.

Not that it mattered now. Not if Jack couldn't find him.

Jack resumed his search, starting in the front gardens of Holly's neighbours. There was no sign of Claude at Kathleen's, or at number 7 or 5. When he reached number 3, the front door opened, and he jumped.

'Just what do you think you're doing?' A big, burly man stood in the doorway. With the light behind him, Jack could only make out his silhouette, not his expression, but he could make a pretty good guess at how unhappy it was anyway. Jack tried to remember if anyone had been home at this house when he stopped by with Claude earlier, but he thought probably not.

He straightened, pulling himself up to his full height but trying to smile in a non-threatening manner. The last thing he needed was to get into a domestic with one of his neighbours. Then he really *would* have to get that transfer in the new year.

'I'm sorry to disturb you, sir. I was just looking for a lost dog.'

The man stepped out into the garden and the street lamp light shone on his face as he frowned. 'A dog? I haven't seen one around. What does he look like?'

'He's a French Bulldog,' Jack explained. 'Short, stocky. Mostly white with ridiculous black ears.'

'Like the one they have across the road?' the man asked.

'That's the one. I'm ... looking after him as a favour.'

'Not very well, by the look of things.' The man motioned him towards the house. 'Come on. You might as well check the back garden while you're here.'

'Thanks.' Jack followed, trying not to sigh. This could

be a very long night if he had to check every garden in the neighbourhood.

On the other hand, at least he was finally talking to his neighbours. That had to count for something, right?

'Are you looking for Claude?' A red-headed teenager girl appeared on the stairs as Jack passed through the hallway, dressed in a jumper covered in sequinned baubles. 'I heard you say you were looking for a dog.'

'You know Claude?' Jack asked, blinking as the Christmas tree lights flashed off the sequins.

'Not personally. But I've been sharing the Find Claude page with all my friends, and they're all looking out for him now too.' She held up a tablet computer as if to demonstrate.

'The … What Find Claude page?' Jack glanced over at the girl's father, but he just shrugged.

'I have no idea of half the things Jessica does on that device,' he admitted. 'Her mother tells me it's all fine, though.'

'Bella McCawley set it up,' Jessica explained. 'They're over in France for Christmas, but Claude escaped from his crate in the boot before they left. They've been trying to get back ever since they realised, once they got on the ferry, but all the boats are cancelled. So she's mobilising social media to help find and look after Claude until they get here. It's pretty clever, actually.'

Claude had escaped. They hadn't abandoned him, or forgotten him. That made far more sense. Jack could just see Claude slipping out and following his nose, just like he'd done tonight.

'Can you get a message to the McCawleys?' he asked, and Jessica nodded. 'Tell them … tell them Claude was fine when I last saw him, about half an hour ago. He's still in Maple Drive somewhere, I think. And I *will* find him, and look after him. Tell them that?'

Jessica nodded. 'Sure. And … who are you?'

'I'm Jack, the postman,' Jack said. 'I live here on Maple Drive.'

'Cool.' Jessica turned and ran back up the stairs, hopefully to pass on his message. And Jack realised he'd just taken another step towards belonging.

CHAPTER
EIGHT

CLAUDE

I watched Jack as he traipsed in and out of the gardens and houses of Maple Drive, calling my name. I should have felt bad about making him search the neighbourhood, but he *had* wanted to send me to the pound. He didn't deserve my sympathy.

It was simple enough to stay out of his way; once he'd gone down one side of the street and switched to the other, I just hung out in the gardens he'd already searched for a while. Eventually, I saw him disappear back down to the end of the road, his shoulders hunched. He'd given up.

I tried to be pleased. That was what I wanted, right? Except now I really was alone. I supposed I could go and squeeze through Perdita's cat flap again if I had to, but that was a path straight to the pound. No, I couldn't risk it. I'd just have to go it alone.

It seemed you couldn't force a family – couldn't force people to belong together, make them a home just by wishing. You had to all *want* to be together. And as much as I wanted to be with Daisy and Oliver and the kids, or even with Jack and Holly and Kathleen, none of them wanted me. And that made my heart ache more than my poor, cold paws.

Standing up and shaking off a few loose leaves from the bush I'd been hiding under, I tried to encourage myself. This was a challenge. A chance to prove that I was more than just a home dog. More than just a pet. I was Claude, intrepid adventurer, capable of surviving the harshest winters, of making my own way in the world, no humans required.

I just wished one of them had left some food out for me. A piece of gingerbread or two, maybe. Just in case this intrepid adventurer got a little peckish.

Someone opened the front door leading out to the garden where I was hiding, and I decided it was time to get adventuring, just in case they spotted me and called Jack. I couldn't let anybody see me, I realised. Jack had spoken to everyone, and the moment anyone saw me they would contact him, and I'd be on my way to the pound. I had to stay hidden, at least until Daisy and Oliver came home.

Staying in the shadows, I trotted along the side of the road, looking for a friendly garden to hide in. It was getting later, and most of the houses were closed up for the night, warm looking lights shining behind their windows. But we intrepid adventurers didn't need indoors, anyway.

We didn't need family.

Right?

DAISY

Mum showed Bella and Jay to their rooms, while Daisy and Oliver got the travel cots set up in their assigned bedroom. It was huge, at least, with plenty of space for the cots, and Mum had put a small, potted Christmas tree on the windowsill, where it moved gently in the breeze from the ill-fitting glass. The four poster bed was strangely shabby, with its moth eaten velvet coverings, and the flat, hard cushions where pillows should be.

Everywhere felt as if it had been half emptied, then abandoned. Daisy wrinkled her nose at the smell of the sheets, and hoped that Jay's room was slightly less Transylvanian gothic, or they were going to find him piled into bed with them in the middle of the night, as well as at least one of the twins.

'What on earth were they thinking, buying this place?' Oliver asked, as he struggled to set up the first travel cot. Daisy crossed the room to take over.

'You find the sheets. I think they're in that bag.' She pointed at the largest case. 'Or possibly that one, actually. And I don't know what they were thinking. I just got a call one day a couple of months ago saying that they'd sold the house and bought this place.'

'Do you think it's some sort of three-quarter life crisis?'

Oliver mused. 'Like, a last ditch attempt to live out their fantasies?'

Daisy stared around her at the dusty stone walls and the crumbling mortar. 'Does this place look much like *anyone's* fantasies?'

'Well, no,' Oliver admitted. 'But you know, the whole moving to a castle in France thing. One of those once in a lifetime opportunities, maybe? Something they figured that if they didn't do it now, they never would?'

Daisy sighed, and sank down onto the bed, a cloud of dust rising around her. 'Perhaps. Do you think my parents are okay with the twins down there?'

'Isn't the question more whether the twins are okay with your parents?' Oliver abandoned his hunt for the sheets and sat beside her on the bed.

'Possibly.'

'Still, it is nice to have a few quiet moments alone, isn't it?' His arm crept around her shoulder. 'And with a four poster bed, to boot.'

Daisy raised an eyebrow at him. 'You absolutely cannot be suggesting what I think you're suggesting.' That sort of thing was how they'd ended up with the twins in the first place. None of their children could really be considered 'planned', but the twins were definitely more accidental than most.

Oliver's arm retreated. 'Fine. Just a thought.'

'We need to call Mrs Templeton, anyway,' Daisy reminded him.

Oliver collapsed back onto the bed with a groan, which quickly turned into a coughing fit as the dust overtook him.

'We need to make sure that Claude's okay, and she's our best shot.' Daisy waited for the coughing to subside, then handed him her phone. 'Go on.'

'Why me?' Oliver asked, staring at the phone in her hand. 'Why can't you do it?'

'She likes you more.'

'She hates me. I mow the lawn too loudly and don't make pretty stripes when I do it.'

'She still likes you more than me. Or any of the kids, for that matter.'

'You don't know that,' Oliver argued. 'You've never actually asked her outright which one of us she hates least.'

'I don't have to,' Daisy said darkly. 'She makes it very clear with her eyes.'

'Yeah, well, she still hates Claude the most.'

That, unfortunately, was true. Mrs Templeton had very little time for animals, Daisy had learnt over several encounters with the old battle-axe, mostly involving her complaining about dogs running wild, dog poo on the pavements, and barking.

Never mind that Claude never ran anywhere if he could help it, or that Daisy paid Bella an extra two quid a week pocket money to pick up after him, or that he rarely barked. Mrs Templeton was not to be reasoned with.

But they were going to have to try.

'Fine,' she said, snatching the phone back. 'I'll do it.'

Oliver looked relieved. 'I'll hold your hand while you call, if you like. For moral support.' Daisy glared at him. 'Or I could check on the twins.'

'That sounds like a much better idea.'

He was gone by the time Daisy had scrolled through her contacts list on her battered old phone and found Mrs Templeton, saved under the obscure title of 'Neighbourhood Witch' instead of her actual name.

The phone rang for what seemed like forever before Mrs Templeton's sharp voice came on the line.

'Hello? Do you realise it's nearly nine o'clock at night? I do hope this is an emergency.'

Daisy sighed. That meant it was nearly ten in France, and she could still hear Jay running around with Petal downstairs. Bedtime was apparently a thing of the past.

'Hello, Mrs Templeton. It's Daisy McCawley from number 11 here. I'm so sorry to bother you so late.' Or at all, really. It wasn't like she'd be calling if she had any other options. 'It's just, we're in France at my parents' house—'

'France? Does that mean I'm going to be charged for receiving international calls? Because, really, Mrs McCawley—'

'No, no, I'm paying for the call,' Daisy reassured her, pretty sure that was true. 'And I wouldn't call if it wasn't important. Only, it's our dog, Claude. We meant to bring him with us, only …' *We managed to bring a soft toy instead. As you do.* God, Mrs Templeton was going to think she was more of an incapable idiot than she already did after this. 'He seems to have escaped from his cage in the car before we left.' That sounded rather more reasonable, Daisy decided.

'And you didn't check? Good grief.' Daisy could just picture Mrs Templeton shaking her head in despair for the younger generation as she spoke. 'So now there is a potentially rabid dog running wild around Maple Drive, thanks to you.'

'Claude isn't rabid!'

'He might not have been when you left, but a lot can change in a day, Mrs McCawley.'

Daisy felt that Claude contracting rabies might be pushing it a little far, though. 'I'm sure Claude is fine, Mrs Templeton. I was just hoping that you might have seen him. I know how you like to keep an eye on goings on in the street.' *Because you're the nosiest woman in the world.*

'As it happens, I did see your creature earlier today, chasing that abominably fluffy cat from number 12.' It was nice to know that Mrs Templeton was equally grumpy towards all animals, Daisy decided. And, more importantly, a relief to know that Claude had been fine when he'd last been seen.

'That's great. I don't suppose you know what happened to him next?'

'I wouldn't have the faintest idea. Now, if you don't mind, I do have my own tasks to be getting on with, rather than trying to find your dog for you …'

'Of course. Sorry,' Daisy said. 'We have set up a page on social media, though. Well, Bella has, and she's monitoring it all the time on her phone. It's called Find Claude. So you're not the only one looking out for him!' For some reason, she felt the overwhelming need to show Mrs Templeton that they were *trying*. That they hadn't just gone away and forgotten about Claude.

'I hardly think that a teenage girl with a phone is going to find a missing dog from several hundred miles away, do you?' Mrs Templeton said.

Daisy deflated. She was right, of course. Find Claude was a start, but it wasn't enough. They had to get home to him.

But until then … 'If you do happen to see him again, do you think you could—'

'If I see him again, now I know you are out of the country, I shall do my civic duty and call the pound directly. Merry Christmas, Mrs McCawley.'

'But—' It was too late; the line had already gone dead.

'I take it that went well?' Oliver asked from the doorway,

Lara in his arms sucking on her dummy.

Daisy sighed as she lowered the phone from her ear. 'How does that woman make "Merry Christmas" sound like a curse?'

'She probably took an extra course at Evil University.' Oliver jiggled Lara around a bit in the sort of way that was never going to get her to sleep. 'So, no sign of Claude?'

'Oh, she saw him all right. Chasing the cat from across the road.'

'Ah. His furry nemesis.'

Daisy rolled her eyes. 'I'm pretty sure Claude is too lazy to have a nemesis.'

'I think you'd be surprised. But he's okay, then?'

'He was, when she saw him. But it does mean he's outside, in the cold.' Poor Claude. He wasn't even wearing his coat.

Oliver sat beside her on the bed, still holding Lara. 'I do miss him, you know. And I *am* worried about him, even if I don't seem it.'

'I know,' Daisy said, even though she hadn't until he said. It was nice to know now, though.

'I don't suppose Mrs Templeton offered to take him in if she sees him again?'

'She's going to call the pound.' Daisy dropped her head to her hands. 'I think I might just have made things even worse. And I wasn't sure that was physically possible.'

'Oh, things can always be worse,' Oliver said, unhelpfully, as Lara started to wail, as if on cue.

'Apparently so,' Daisy agreed, taking the baby from him. 'But one thing is certain. We need to get home. As soon as possible.'

Claude would never forgive them if they didn't. If he was even still there when they made it back.

HOLLY

Her new outdoor lights wouldn't arrive until the next morning, and Holly didn't want to put the icicles back up before they came in case Mrs Templeton came over to complain again. Far better to spring the whole display on her at once, Holly had decided. But she did want to decorate *something*, and with the tree already up, and every room made suitably festive, that only left Perdita.

Perdita was not enjoying the experience, Holly could tell.

Finally, once she'd wrestled the cat into her Christmas jumper, set a tiny Santa hat on her head, and taken a few photos for her blog, Holly gave up.

'Oh, okay. Go find a nice warm radiator to curl up on, then,' Holly said, and Perdita took her chance at escape, the Santa hat toppling off as she darted up the stairs.

Holly looked around at her living room. The tree was lit with beautiful bright white lights, and decorated in a perfect red and white colour scheme. A green garland rested on the mantlepiece, and a cinnamon-scented candle burned on the side table. She had a glass of mulled wine, and Christmas music playing through the telly. What else could she possibly need?

She sighed. She needed something to *do*. Something to make her feel useful, and wanted and part of something.

Something to make her feel less alone.

Something to distract her from the fact that she'd spent most of this year expecting to be preparing for her wedding tomorrow.

She couldn't help but think about it. Even knowing she was well rid of Sebastian, she couldn't help but visualise her wedding dress hanging on the back of the door: snowy white lace and a beautiful chiffon skirt, adorned with tiny diamond-like jewels that sparkled in the candlelight. She'd have been sipping prosecco with her friends, her mother and Sebastian's sisters. Her engagement ring would still be heavy on her left hand, and she'd be feeling relaxed from the pampering day that Sebastian would have given her as a treat.

They'd probably have been doing all the last tiny touches tonight – tying ribbons on the handmade menus and the Order of Service handout she'd designed, finishing off the individual favours she'd made. It would all have been personal and crafty and perfect – and what world was she living in, exactly?

Holly took another swig of mulled wine, and forced herself to face reality.

Sebastian would have insisted on ordering all the wedding stationery and favours and stuff from John Lewis, and he'd never have thought to book her a pampering day in a million years. Her mother would be sick with nerves, Sebastian's sisters would *never* have spent the evening here, and she didn't even *like* prosecco all that much.

Most importantly, she'd have been making a huge mistake.

With Sebastian out of her life, she got to be herself again. To focus on the things she loved – her craft business, Christmas, Perdita.

And she got to do it all alone.

Holly sighed. At least there was the prospect of seeing Jack tomorrow, even if it was only because he wanted to surprise the lady next door with a Christmas treat. She had to keep that in mind when he was there, and not let herself get distracted by his lovely arms, or his nice smile, or those eyes ...

No. She was not going to spend the evening fantasising about the postman. That was simply a level of pathetic-ness she was not willing to stoop to.

But she needed to do *something* to take her mind off the fact that the only guy she'd had the slightest spark with since Sebastian left had told her flat out that he was leaving soon. At least he'd had the decency to give her fair warning, before she got invested. It was more than Sebastian had done.

Restless, Holly got to her feet and moved across the room, switching the song playing to something more upbeat and less slow and smoochy Christmas. She needed excitement. Energy. Action.

Maybe she could do some preparation for Kathleen's Christmas surprise. Show Jack that she was involved for the right reasons too – not just because she wanted to flirt with him. That had to be a good start, right? But what? The decorations were already ordered, it was too late to go food shopping, she'd already made enough bunting and napkins and table cloths to host three Christmases and ... The cake!

Dashing out of the lounge, Holly yanked open the under stairs cupboard and pulled out the tin she'd hidden away at the bottom of a box two months ago, only pulling it out periodically to top it up with brandy. How could she have forgotten the Christmas cake? She'd made it in a fit of despair after Sebastian had left, and then put it away and not given it another thought. If she hadn't been desperate for distraction tonight, she might not have remembered to decorate it at all!

Taking the tin through to the kitchen she cleared a space for it on the table and set it out. It smelled heavenly, and she had so many ideas already about decorations. The marzipan and icing were all ready and waiting, too.

Holly frowned. The only thing was, it didn't look so big, now. Understandably; when she'd made it, she'd assumed she'd be alone for Christmas. Other than the possible friend or two popping by there was no one else to eat it anyway. But now ... it looked sort of sad and small. There was probably plenty for her and Jack and Kathleen, though. And Claude, if he came back.

But what if some of the other people on the street stopped by? Or maybe a colleague from school might pop in for coffee, sometime between Christmas and New Year. She'd need extra cake then, right?

It was too late to make another fruit cake. But an extra tier of a plain sponge cake wouldn't take very long. And maybe a chocolate tier too, just in case. And obviously some extra decorations to go with it ...

Suddenly Holly's mind spun with all the possibilities, and she reached for her apron without even thinking.

Maybe Jack wasn't staying, and maybe spending Christmas with the postman and the neighbour she'd only exchanged a few words with in almost a year was the official definition of pathetic. It didn't matter.

This was *her* Christmas – her first Christmas in her new home, her first Christmas without Sebastian.

And she was going to make it truly epic.

Starting with cake.

CHAPTER
NINE

CLAUDE

On Maple Drive, every house was lit except my own. Inside each of those other houses, behind those closed curtains, I knew there would be Christmas trees and fairy lights and probably gingerbread.

But out here, there was only cold and loneliness.

I stumbled to the end of the street, and stared up at the garden there. In the middle of the lawn was a low wooden table, beside a larger one that looked like a tiny house on a stick. Bird tables, I realised. Humans left food for the birds sometimes, didn't they? I'd seen Daisy throw out old crusts onto the grass at our house for the sparrows, sometimes.

Cat food hadn't been all that different from dog food, but I suspected that bird food might be a different matter altogether.

Still, intrepid adventurers had to take food where they could find it, right?

Sniffing, I approached the lower table, hoping there might be some tasty treats there to try. Maybe birds liked gingerbread too. But all I found was some seeds and nuts, and a few small scraps of bread. I snuffled unhappily, then tried them anyway.

Not good. Not good at all.

'What are you doing, you hideous creature?' The screeching

voice came from the doorstep. I glanced up and saw Mrs Templeton standing in the open door, waving a fist at me.

This was worse than bird food.

Turning tail, I raced next door, back into my own, familiar garden. At least no one could find me there. It was my home.

'I'm calling the pound!' Mrs Templeton cried behind me, and I tried to run faster, desperate to get away, but my little legs could only move so fast.

Fortunately, it was still faster than Mrs Templeton.

I collapsed a few moments later at the foot of the tree holding Jay's tree house, and let out a long, sad wail.

Why wouldn't they come home? Where *were* they? What was so wonderful about France, ferry and chateau that they had to stay away and leave me here alone?

'You really are a mess, aren't you?' Perdita sprang lightly from the treehouse down to the lower branches, then to the ground in front of me.

'At least I don't have to wear a Christmas jumper,' I growled back.

Perdita swung her tail lazily from side to side. 'At least my owner cares enough to buy me one. Where are yours again? Oh yes, gone away. Without you.'

'Because I was chasing you!' I knew they wouldn't have left me behind otherwise. Would they?

'Are you sure that's the only reason? Then why haven't they come back?' She shook her head, her bright green eyes shining in the night. 'Face it, dog. Your family don't want you any more. You are officially an abandoned dog.'

No. No, I wouldn't believe it. 'Holly fed me. Jack was looking for me. I have people who want me.'

'But you're hiding from them out here. Why is that again?'

Perdita asked. 'Let me guess ... they wanted to send you to the pound.'

'How did you know that?'

'I heard them talking too.' She gave me a long steady look. 'Maybe you should go. At least they might give you a decent last meal there.'

I lunged forward, putting all my weight and force into my muscles to shock her, swiping out with one paw. She darted back out of the way with a yowl, but I got close enough to know she was scared. 'Get out of my garden,' I barked. 'And don't come back.'

She dashed away, scaling the fence in a moment. Pausing on the top, she turned back and hissed down at me. 'You mark my words. It won't be your garden for very long.'

'You're wrong,' I said, but she was already gone, down over the fence and away to her own home, and Holly, and warmth and food.

I huddled down at the base of the tree and tried to get warm. 'You're wrong,' I muttered to myself again. 'They're coming back for me.'

I just wished I could believe my own words.

Outside, the world at night was very different to my cosy bed inside number 11 Maple Drive.

As I huddled under the tree in the back garden, my paws around my head, I tried to sleep, to rest, but I couldn't.

First, it was the noises keeping me awake. Strange, unfamiliar noises that I never heard during the day. Hoots and snaps and whistles and even a strange bark, that didn't sound like any dog I'd ever met.

Then my stomach started to rumble.

Normally, inside, there'd be a little something in my bowl

for me to snack on, just in case this happened. Oliver always made sure of it before he went to bed – even though I'd heard Daisy tell him not to, that I ate plenty during the day. (Surely, if I ate plenty during the day I wouldn't be hungry during the night, right?) But Oliver wasn't there. None of them were.

And I was outside.

Even Perdita had disappeared inside for the night. I thought about sneaking back in through her cat flap, but the fear of Holly finding me and calling the pound was too great. So instead, I stayed huddled at the base of Jay's treehouse, wishing my family would come home.

It was the longest night ever.

DAISY

Eventually, Jay and the twins were asleep, and even Bella was curled up with her Kindle in her room.

'It's kind of cool here, I suppose,' Bella had said doubtfully when Daisy stopped by to tuck her in, even though she was fourteen and convinced she didn't need it. 'Dusty, but cool.'

'I suppose.' Daisy had perched on the end of her bed. 'But you'd rather be home for Christmas, wouldn't you?'

Bella had given her best 'how did you survive so long being this dumb' look and said, 'Well, yeah.'

Which was pretty much how Daisy felt about the situation too. And that feeling only grew when her father took her on a tour of the chateau.

'And down here, we have the wine cellar! Mind the steps, though, there's a few missing.'

'Of course there are,' Daisy muttered, as she followed him into the cellar, testing each step before she put any weight on it. 'Dad, do you really think this chateau is the best place for you? I mean, at your time of life?'

'Careful, Daisy. That could almost count as being ageist.' Dad pulled a filthy light pull and a bare bulb lit up above them. 'Now, where did I put that nice bottle of Châteauneuf-du-Pape? Seems appropriate, no?'

'Very. And I'm not being ageist.' Just realistic. 'This place would be a huge challenge for anybody. It could take decades to get it into shape.'

'Are you implying we don't have decades left?'

Daisy sighed, and bit back on the impulse to remind her dad that he was already sixty-nine and had had two heart attacks in the last five years. 'I hope you have much, much longer, Dad, you know that. I'm just not sure why you'd want to spend them over here, so far from your family, trying to keep this place from falling down around your ears.'

'But, darling, don't you think it's romantic?' her mum asked, from halfway down the stairs behind her. Great. One of them she might have been able to reason with. But both of them … impossible. It was like the crazy fed off each other. And where was Oliver? Why wasn't he helping her with this conversation?

Probably because his parents were perfectly ordinary pensioners, and very happy with their semi in the suburbs. He never had known how to deal with her parents. Of course, neither had she, really. If she had, maybe she could have stopped this crazy plan before it got as far as needing passports to visit. And possibly hard hats.

'Romantic?' Daisy asked, thinking about the four poster bed upstairs. 'I suppose it has its charms, but really …'

'Not the building! The adventure!' Mum skipped down the steps like a woman half Daisy's age, avoiding the missing step without a problem. 'That's what we wanted! A big project for me and your dad to take on together. To bring us closer, now we're both retired.'

Ah. Suddenly this was all starting to make more sense. 'To bring you closer together?' she asked, sceptically. 'Or was it

164

more because you didn't know what to do with yourselves once you were both rattling around at home together?'

Her parents exchanged a look, and Daisy knew she'd hit the nail on the proverbial head. 'You were bored, weren't you?' she guessed. 'You were bored, and tetchy, and bickering, and you couldn't just take up ballroom dancing like everyone else's parents.'

'Your father has two left feet,' Mum pointed out. 'Besides, this is much more exciting.'

Daisy leant against the wall of the wine cellar and tried to figure out how her life had come to this. As if wrangling four children wasn't enough, now she had to do it for her parents as well.

'Although, I have to admit, there is rather more work involved than the advertisement led us to believe,' Dad said.

'Let me guess. You found an advert for a real, French chateau in the back of one of the Sunday papers, right? What did it say? In need of some refurbishment?'

Mum sniffed. 'It said – perfectly accurately, you have to admit – that it was ripe and ready for some dedicated couple to put their stamp on it.'

'That it is,' Daisy conceded. 'So they didn't mention the crumbling plaster or the fact that the ceiling is missing in the second sitting room?'

'Not exactly,' Dad said. 'No. It didn't mention the collared doves that keep flying down through the chimney in the kitchen, either.'

'Or the bats.' Daisy shuddered.

'But it was a bargain,' Mum argued. 'Really, Daisy, they were practically giving it away.'

'I can't imagine why.' Probably the previous owners just

wanted to get out before the whole place collapsed around their ears.

Time to try reason and logic. Admittedly, they'd never worked with her parents before, but there was a first time for everything. 'Look, we're going to have to go back for Claude tomorrow, as long as we can get space on the ferry. Why don't you come with us? We can all have Christmas together at Maple Drive. Where we're less likely to be brained by falling battlements.'

'Daisy,' Dad said sternly.

'Did I say that last part out loud? Sorry. It's been a very long day.' She tried to smile encouragingly. 'All I'm saying is, if things aren't quite ready here for guests, that's fine. We need to head home anyway. And you're very welcome to join us.'

There was silence as her parents had one of those silent conversations involving hand gestures and facial movements that they'd always done whenever they were pretending not to argue in front of her when she was a child. God, she did that with Oliver now, didn't she? She really was turning into her mother. Except her mother had only had one child to deal with. That was practically cheating.

'Well, maybe,' Mum said, eventually. 'We'll think about it.'

'And see if the oven blows again next time we try to use it,' Dad added.

'That might be the deciding factor,' Mum admitted.

'That or one of those blasted doves pooing on my head again,' Dad grumbled.

'Great,' Daisy said, wishing she felt brighter about it than she did. 'I'll call the ferry company.'

All she needed now was six places – and two baby spaces – for the only ferry home on Christmas Eve. The fully booked only ferry home.

How hard could that be?

'Season of miracles,' she muttered under her breath, as she climbed back out of the cellar, almost falling through the gap in the stairs. 'And, Dad? Bring the wine.'

JACK

Jack let himself into his tiny two-up, two-down terrace house, on the corner of Maple Drive, and realised, not for the first time, how empty it was.

Maybe it was just after spending time in Holly's exceptionally festive house, or with Kathleen and all her souvenirs from her travels, but tonight it felt worse than ever. He didn't let himself consider the fact that it might just be that he was missing Claude.

Dropping his coat onto the back of the sofa, he headed for the kitchen and a rarely used cupboard, where he remembered stashing a bag of Christmas decorations he'd bought from the supermarket on a whim a few weeks ago, then never got around to putting up. Perhaps a bit of festive cheer might perk the place up a bit.

Twenty minutes later, he had a miniature fake tree on his side table in the lounge, decorated with tiny bulbs of different colours, a garland of plastic greenery hanging over the bannister, and a wreath made of brightly coloured baubles to welcome him home every time he opened his front door. It might not be a patch on Holly's homemade Christmas decorations, but it was enough for him.

For now, anyway.

One day, he wanted all that – the huge, real tree in the front room with a stack of presents under it for all the occupants of the house, the friends stopping by unannounced for mince pies and mulled wine, even the light-up Santa on the roof. But despite the day's adventures, he still couldn't see himself finding that in Maple Drive.

He'd thought, just for a moment, that there might be a spark of a chance between him and Holly. She was beautiful, funny, incredibly talented and, more than any of that, he'd felt a connection to her. A flash that showed him there was something in their souls that matched. It wasn't just that she was lost and alone, the same as him, although he supposed that was part of it. But more than that, he'd looked into her eyes and felt, for the first time since he'd left the army, that here was someone who could matter to him. Who he could matter to.

And then she'd pulled away, and that moment had been over.

Well, he supposed he couldn't blame her. She was clearly still hung up on her ex, whatever she said. She might not want the guy himself any more – and she'd be crazy if she did, from what Jack had heard – but the idea of it. She was supposed to be getting married tomorrow, supposed to be starting a whole new life. It had to be hard to make the sudden adjustment to another possibility.

Raiding the fridge for a beer, Jack settled down on his sofa and pulled out his laptop. He couldn't spend all night obsessing about the pretty blonde at number 12 – he had an appointment to keep.

The video call ringtone was annoying as hell, but fortunately Tom didn't let it ring too long.

'Jack, buddy! Merry Christmas Eve, Eve!' Tom's voice

boomed out across the thousands of miles between them, and Jack felt something in his shoulders relax at the sound of it. Maybe the reason he hadn't found a new home, new people, was that he knew he couldn't beat the one he'd left behind.

He didn't regret leaving the army. But he did regret leaving his best friend, his family, behind when he resigned.

'How's it going over there?' Jack asked, before Tom could start in with his usual questions about how Jack was adjusting to civilian life. He didn't want to talk about himself today – especially since Tom's questions were usually about whether or not Jack had a girlfriend yet. He wanted to pretend he was back there, in the middle of it all, with Tom and the others.

'Oh, you know,' Tom said, evasively. 'Same old, same old.'

'You mean you can't talk about it,' Jack guessed.

'Definitely not over this connection, no.' Jack knew it wasn't the connection that was the problem. It was his non-military status.

That stung. Once, Jack would have known everything Tom did, the minute he knew it. Once, that would have been his life, his adventure, too. But now he was on the outside, looking in, unable to be part of the life Tom led.

'What about the boys, then? Any news?' News, in this case, meant gossip. Tom was worse than Mrs Templeton for gossiping about the guys they served with.

But Tom's face turned sober. 'We lost Graham,' he said, eyes heavy. 'I'm sorry, mate.'

Graham. Young, excitable, ready to live life to the fullest Graham.

'That ... God. That sucks.' There were stronger words, deeper words, and Jack knew he'd use all of them later, alone. But for now, all he could do was rely on the fact that Tom knew him well enough to know how badly that news hurt.

'Yeah. It's … quieter without him.'

'It would be,' Jack said, a half joke, an almost smile. Just like Graham would have wanted. 'Can you give me details?'

'Some,' Tom said. Jack listened as Tom detailed Graham's last days, last minutes, and took it in. Another loss, another story to retell among friends, when they came home.

And he felt further away than ever.

'But enough about us,' Tom said, in the end, after a lengthy pause where they just stared at their respective screens and remembered. 'Seriously, what's been going on there? How's Operation Find A Family going?'

There were times when Jack really regretted getting drunk and telling Tom all about his hopes for civilian life. But at least, he supposed, it meant he had someone to keep him on track, or call him out when the steps he was taking weren't getting him closer to his dreams.

'I put in a request for that transfer we talked about,' Jack said. 'My boss told me to think it over some more.'

'What's there to think about? If the place you are doesn't have what you're looking for, it's time to move on.' Tom sounded so definite, so certain, that Jack couldn't help but agree with him. 'Life's too short to waste time somewhere that isn't where you're meant to be. Isn't that what you told me when you left?'

'Yeah, I did.'

'And you were right,' Tom said. 'Just look at Graham.'

'Yeah.' Jack's doubt must have sounded in his voice, because Tom sighed.

'Okay, what's changed?' he asked. 'Because last time we talked, you were on your way out of there. What's making you think twice? Your boss?'

'Maybe a little. But mostly …' What was it, exactly, that had him thinking about changing his mind? Was it Holly, with her sparkly cat lead, craft fixation and love of Christmas? Or was it Kathleen, so alone after all her moving around? Or was it everything that had happened that day, all rolled into one?

When he thought about his day, Jack remembered not feeling so lonely, for the first time in months. Remembered feeling, even just for a moment, like he belonged. He closed his eyes for a second and pictured what it was that had given him that feeling, and to his surprise he saw a black nose on a white muzzle, covered in gingerbread crumbs, under oversized bat ears and black patched eyes.

Claude. He was what had started it all. And that was why he had to find him, whatever else happened on Maple Drive this Christmas. He had to find Claude and make sure he was okay.

Jack opened his eyes and grinned at his friend over the video call. 'Okay, so this is going to sound weird. But it started with this dog doing a belly flop through a cat flap …'

CHAPTER
TEN

DAISY

Daisy stepped out through the back door, leaving it to creak closed behind her, and let out a long sigh. Resting against the outside wall, she tipped her head against the cold stone and tried to calm her racing mind.

Then she realised she wasn't alone.

'Hello?' she called, her muscles tensing as she tried to make out the edges of the form in the shadows. 'Um, *bonjour*? Or, *bonne nuit*, I suppose?'

A familiar, world-weary sigh came from the shadows, and Bella held up her phone to illuminate her face. 'It's me, Mum.'

'Of course it is.' Daisy pressed a hand to her chest in the hope it might calm her racing heart. 'I knew that. I was just … practising my French.'

She couldn't *see* Bella roll her eyes in the darkness, but she could feel it, all the same.

'What are you doing out here?' Daisy asked, stepping closer. Bella had found an old picnic table, and was sat on the bench, her knees against her chest, her back resting against a wall. 'I thought you'd gone to bed.'

'No signal in there.' Bella tapped the screen of her smartphone again. 'I thought I'd try out here.'

'Any better?' Daisy tried not to dwell on the roaming

charges. Out here, in the darkness, in a strange country … maybe this was one of those perfect bonding moments. A mother and daughter moment in time where they could confess all their secrets to each other.

Or, at the least, maybe Bella would finally tell her why she was so bloody grumpy about spending Christmas in France.

'A little,' Bella said. 'I managed to pick up a message from Jessica.'

'Jessica?' Daisy had to think for a moment. 'Oh! At number 3! Did she have any news on Claude?'

Bella nodded. 'She's putting up Find Claude posters tomorrow. Oh, and apparently the postman has been going door to door searching everyone's gardens for him. He said to tell us that that he was fine when he last spotted him, and that he *will* find him.'

'The postman?' Daisy frowned. Why on earth did the *postman* care?

'Apparently,' Bella said, with a shrug.

'Is that all?' Apart from the very nice bottle of French something or other she would have to buy the postman on the ferry. It was the least she could do.

'Yeah.'

'But you're still out here because …?' Daisy let it dangle there, waiting for Bella to fill in the blanks.

'I wanted to send a text message.'

'Oh?' £1.50, Daisy's mind calculated automatically, apparently channelling Oliver. 'Who to?'

Bella's eyes slid away, back down to the black screen.

'Bell? Who were you texting?' Daisy pressed, feeling the first prickles of panic. Just when she was slightly reassured that Claude would be okay, now she was fretting about Bella.

Obviously she was texting someone she didn't want her to know about. Which meant a boy, surely. Or a man. Bella was fourteen now, and Daisy actively shuddered to remember all the things she'd got up to at that age and never told her parents about.

God, what if it was some thirty-something she'd met on the internet? What if Bella was being groomed right under her nose and she never noticed because she was knee deep in dirty nappies and dog poo. And, really, why was her life *all* about poo these days anyway?

Back to the more important issue.

'You can tell me, you know,' she said, as calmly as she could manage. 'You can tell me anything. You know it will never make me love you any less.'

Another eye roll. 'I know *that*, Mum.'

'Well, good. Then, who was it?'

'It's private.'

Definitely something funky going on. Perhaps she should call Oliver out here too. Maybe they could get a private detective to seize her phone records. And her computer. And watch her after school.

'Oh God, you're freaking out, aren't you?' Bella dropped her feet to the floor either side of the bench and sat up.

'No,' Daisy lied. 'I'm just considering rational next steps.'

'Fine. I'll tell you.'

Daisy blinked. That was easier than she'd expected. Maybe this wasn't such a disaster after all. 'Great. So, who?'

'Zach.'

She'd been right! It was a boy. One point to motherly instinct. Except …

'Wait. Who's Zach?'

'You know. Zach Templeton.' She said it with the complete lack of patience she always had when Daisy couldn't quite keep up with her rapidly changing friends list. But it didn't matter; Daisy still couldn't place him in the running class list she tried to keep in her head. There was Zachary Rubinstein, who'd moved away when Bella was five, but she doubted that was who Bella meant.

'Zach … wait, Mrs Templeton's grandson?' Daisy tried to picture him, but all she got was an image of weirdly shaped hair peeking out from under a Santa hat. Mrs Templeton's son and daughter-in-law only visited briefly at Christmas and Easter – for which Daisy couldn't blame them at all. 'When did you even get to know him?'

Bella shrugged. 'He was at that lame Easter egg hunt you made me take Jay to. He had to take his little sister. We talked.'

'That was nine months ago!'

'So? We connected. We chat online sometimes, that sort of thing. And I was going to be seeing him this week, until *you* decided to drag us all the way across Europe.'

'We crossed the English Channel,' Daisy pointed out. 'It's about three hundred miles. The north of Scotland is further. We're hardly on the other side of the world.'

'It's not Maple Drive, though.'

And there, Daisy had to admit, she had a point.

'If it makes you feel any better, I'm still trying to get us home tomorrow.' She shuffled closer, stretching an arm out around Bella's rigid shoulders.

'Because of Claude. Not me.' Bella's knees came back up, and she wrapped her arms around them, folding herself like an origami person. 'You care more about what the dog wants than what I want.'

'Be fair, Bella. I didn't know about Zach.' Although she should have. How could her daughter have been carrying on an online flirtation with the neighbour's grandson for nine months, without her noticing? Maybe they should hire than private detective after all.

'You knew I didn't want to come here, though,' Bella said, accusingly.

Daisy sighed. 'Bell, *none* of us wanted to come here. We all think this is utterly crazy.'

'Then why did we?'

'Because we love your grandparents,' Daisy said simply. 'And because Christmas is a time to be with the people you love.' *Oh God, please don't say you're in love with Zach Templeton.* She wasn't sure her heart could take it.

'I suppose,' Bella said, not sounding entirely convinced. 'So, what are we going to do when we go home, then? Take Granny and Grandad with us?'

'That's the plan,' Daisy said.

'That could be nice.'

Bella twisted around on the bench, so her back was against Daisy, and rested her head on her shoulder. Daisy kissed the top of her head and wrapped her arms tighter around her daughter.

One crisis averted.

She glanced down at Bella's phone on the table, flashing the time. Nearly midnight, French time. Nearly Christmas Eve.

How many more crises could there be before Christmas Day?

CLAUDE

By the time the sun came up the next morning, I was freezing cold, lonelier than ever and, most importantly, starving. My poor tummy felt hollow, and I was starting to think that my tiny tail might never wag again.

I shook the dirt and grass from my body and trotted out from my shelter under the tree, looking for a patch of sunlight that might warm me even a little. Then, I knew, it was time to find some food.

Once upon a time, my ancestors might have been natural hunters, but I suspected it must have been a *very* long time ago. Why hunt, when you can adopt a human to provide food for you, after all? We dogs have always been the smartest of creatures, and my breed was smarter than most. Hunting was a thing of the past.

Except all of a sudden, it was a very necessary part of my present. And I had no idea how to go about it.

I decided to start by doing what I always did: follow my nose. My nose had led me to gingerbread yesterday, and my cunning had got me through Perdita's cat flap and fed by Holly. It might not be hunting in the most classic of senses – and I was fairly sure that Perdita would turn up her tail at it and scoff – but it worked for me.

Maple Drive was waking up, and there were all sorts of interesting smells starting to rise out of the houses. Curtains were open, and I could see Christmas trees behind the windows. I frowned as I plodded along the pavement. The problem was, few of the people inside the houses would welcome me in to share their food, even if I could find a way inside. I needed something more accessible.

I started with the bins, round the back of number 10, but they were too high up for me to climb into, and the cat from number 8 sat above me laughing at my every attempt, so I quickly moved on. There was another bird table at number 8, but I skipped that, remembering how awful the bird seed at Mrs Templeton's had tasted. At number 6, I found a small wooden structure with a bowl of what smelled like Perdita's cat food inside it, and tried to force my head through the tiny opening to get to it – until a man came out of the house waving his arms and shouting.

'Oi! That's for the hedgehogs!'

As if hedgehogs needed it more than me, I grumbled, as I hurried back round to the front of the house, and carried on along the pavement, trotting as fast as my little legs would carry me.

Eventually, I reached the end of Maple Drive, and found myself at the gates of Jay's school. The gates were locked, (they'd broken up for holidays the week before, and Jay had been around all the time since. It had been brilliant) but the bars were widely spaced, and it didn't take *too* much wiggling for me to squeeze through. At least if there was any food hiding here, it was unlikely that anyone would be there to chase me away from it.

The playground where Daisy left Jay in the mornings, while I was tied up by the gate, was quiet and deserted, and felt like a different place altogether. I padded past the main school buildings, enjoying for a moment the experience of being somewhere I was never allowed before. It was interesting to see where Jay spent his days, when he couldn't be with me. But really, the place seemed kind of boring. No wonder he always begged to stay home and play instead.

Eventually, I found myself in a big field, open and perfect for running. Why on earth weren't dogs allowed here? It was ideal for us.

The grass was white and frosty under my paws, crunching with every step, and I leapt along to try to stay warm. And then I smelt it.

It was faint, but then I *do* have a hunter's nose, even if it hadn't been used for a few generations. It smelt hidden, and deep, and just a little bit like gingerbread.

I had to find it.

I tracked the smell to the edge of the field, underneath a heavy, old tree, its bare branches swaying in the wind. And then I started to dig, deep down through the roots.

The ground was hard and cold, but the winter sun shining on the patch I was digging helped. As I fought my way through the frozen soil, the scent grew stronger. Warmer.

Tastier.

Then my paws hit something hard – something that didn't look like it would be nice to bite at all. The smell had to be coming from inside it. If I could only find a way in ...

'Claude?'

I froze at the sound of my name, then jumped around to see Holly crossing the field towards me, her bright red coat wrapped tight around her.

I'd been found. And I knew what that meant.

It was time to run again.

HOLLY

'Claude? Claude!' Holly called again, as the little dog scampered through the trees towards the school's back gate. She tried to give chase, but his little body – while not fast – was at least capable of squeezing through spots she couldn't even see.

She stopped, under the tree where Claude had been digging, and wondered what to do next. Should she call Jack, tell him she'd had a Claude sighting? She'd only come by the school because she realised she'd left a bag full of books in the staff room, and had forgotten that the caretaker was away from Christmas Eve and the building wouldn't be open.

Well, no, that wasn't quite true. She'd come out for a walk because she hadn't been getting into her wedding dress, and she'd already decorated the Christmas cake, and she was desperately afraid she might have actually reached the end of all her possible planned Christmas crafts.

Basically, it was Christmas Eve and she no idea what to do until Jack came by to organise Kathleen's Christmas surprise, so she'd got herself out of the house she'd bought with Sebastian and into the fresh air for a change. And then she'd spotted Claude over the railings and, well, everyone in the area knew that the gates at Forest Green First and Middle School were easy enough to unlock, if you knew the trick. So she'd let herself in and followed.

What had he been doing here? Knowing what little she did of Claude, looking for food. But why had he thought he'd find it here? And what had he been digging for?

At least all the questions meant she wasn't thinking about her non-wedding any more.

Holly crouched down on the frozen ground and studied the hole Claude had been digging. Was there something in it? Yes. Something tarnished and battered – but with a tiny bit of sparkle shining through. What on earth had attracted Claude to it, though?

Reaching in, Holly pulled out the object – a tin, she realised. An old fashioned, oversized biscuit tin, maybe, or something similar. Brushing the dirt off it, she shivered. It was too cold to stand about wondering what it was; she'd take it home and figure it out there. And if she was lucky, maybe Claude would come flopping through her cat flap again to find it.

Maple Drive was deserted as she walked back up towards her house – except for the courier delivery van parking at the end of the cul-de-sac.

'My decorations!' Holly gasped, and picked up her pace – but too late. As she reached the path to her house, she spotted the card sticking out of her letterbox. The van's engine started behind her and she turned to wave at the driver, but he just pointed backwards. Towards number 13. Mrs Templeton's house.

Holly grabbed the card from the letterbox. There it was, in scrawled black ink. *Parcel left with neighbour at 13.* Damn it. This never happened when Jack was delivering her orders.

Marshalling her courage, Holly marched straight over to number 13, praying that the decorations she'd ordered had been delivered in some discreet, brown packaging, like they did with orders from Ann Summers and expensive lingerie shops. Not that she'd know, except for her brief research into wedding lingerie.

But she could tell from Mrs Templeton's face as she opened the door that this wasn't going to be the case.

'I suppose you're looking for *these*.' Mrs Templeton spat the last word as she pointed at the pile of parcels, all proudly emblazoned with the words 'The UK's Premier Outdoor Christmas Decoration Company!'

Not subtle.

Good grief, how many had she ordered? She'd sort of lost track after the first few pages of adding things to her online basket ... but it looked like she'd bought enough decorations to cover all of Maple Drive, never mind her little house.

'Thank you for taking them in for me, Mrs Templeton,' Holly said, in her best sweet-schoolteacher voice. 'I'll take them off your hands right away.'

'Wait a moment, young lady,' Mrs Templeton said. 'Don't you play me for a fool. I know what you're doing. There are more decorations in these boxes, aren't there? After I specifically informed you that they were not allowed on Maple Drive!'

She could claim she'd ordered them before their conversation the day before, Holly realised. Promise that she was going to send them straight back where they came from, and go forth and decorate no more. She could appease Mrs Templeton the way she appeased everyone – the way she had Sebastian, going out of her way to make his life easier, to help him relax after a hard day at the office, or forgiving him instantly for all those late nights he had to work and forgot to tell her about. She could assume the blame, the guilt, and leave Mrs Templeton mollified.

Or she could take back Christmas.

Holly glanced down at the epic stack of boxes. They might not be to everyone's taste, but she had ordered those decorations because *she* liked them. Because they made her feel festive, and happy, and she wanted the house she'd struggled to make a home for one after Sebastian left feel as if it really did belong to her after all. She'd paid for them with her own money, earned from her little online shop after her teacher's salary had all gone on boring things, like the mortgage. She'd worked for those decorations.

She deserved those decorations, and the happiness they would bring her.

'Actually, Mrs Templeton,' she said, straightening her spine. 'I checked the resident's charter that you gave me when I moved in. Not only does it not appear to be in any way an official document, but there is no mention of Christmas decorations anywhere in it.'

'An oversight,' Mrs Templeton snapped. 'Probably because before *you* moved to this street, it never needed to be spelt out! Nobody would *dream*—'

'Well, I dreamed,' Holly interrupted. She didn't have to listen to this. 'In fact, I did more than dream. I ordered. And now I am going to decorate.' She slammed the tin Claude had discovered down on top of the boxes, and bent down to lift the whole stack. 'Merry Christmas, Mrs Templeton.' And with that, she nodded sharply, and prepared to make her grand exit.

'Wait!'

Holly sighed. So much for a clean getaway. 'Mrs Templeton, it's my house! I can decorate it any way I want, and the Neighbourhood Watch has no right to tell me otherwise!'

'Never mind the stupid decorations.' Mrs Templeton

reached out to run a finger over the top of the tin. 'Where on earth did you find *that*?'

Holly blinked, and shifted her arms around the boxes to get a better grip. 'The tin? Claude was digging it up on the school field.'

'The school field …' For a moment, Mrs Templeton looked misty-eyed and far away, something Holly had felt secure in saying would never happen, five minutes ago. Then she snapped back to the present. 'Give it to me,' she demanded.

'No!' Holly's refusal was automatic, instinctive. 'Why should I?'

'Because it's mine.'

'If it belongs to anyone, it belongs to the school.'

'*My* school. I was headmistress there for twenty years, long before you came along you realise, and *I* buried that tin there. It is mine.'

'*You* buried it?' Holly paused to give a moment's thanks that Mrs Templeton had retired long before she began teaching at Forest Green School. It was hard to imagine they'd view the profession in quite the same way. 'Then, what is it?'

'A time capsule,' Mrs Templeton said. 'A Christmas time capsule, buried twenty-five years ago this Christmas.'

'A Christmas time capsule?' Holly stared at the tin with a new appreciation. 'That's a brilliant idea.' She'd have to try it with her class next year.

'Of course it is.' Mrs Templeton's voice didn't contain a hint of modesty. 'I love Christmas, and I wanted my students to love it too.'

Mrs Templeton loves Christmas. Who'd have thought it?

'Well then.' Holly adjusted her stack of boxes again. 'Don't you think it's time we opened your time capsule?'

CHAPTER ELEVEN

CLAUDE

As the day wore on, I watched from the shadows as people moved around Maple Drive. The redheaded girl at number 3 walked up and down the street sticking some sort of paper sheets onto the lampposts, but she wasn't my focus.

My focus was Holly. She'd spotted me, she'd found my shiny box, and I wanted to know what she was going to do next.

Holly carried my shiny box across to Mrs Templeton's house, then back to her own – along with many other boxes – Mrs Templeton following. I'd never thought them to be friends before, but apparently they had something they were working on together right now.

I just really hoped it wasn't finding me and sending me to the pound.

But really, what else could it be? What else could those two women have in common?

Perhaps it was time to leave Maple Drive, before the worst happened. I'd believed that Jack and Holly were my friends, that they would take care of me until Daisy, Oliver and the children came home. But now I knew they were just as likely to turn me in as Mrs Templeton was. And probably the guy whose hedgehog food I'd eaten.

I could hide out in another neighbourhood, I supposed.

One where no one knew me, or who I belonged to – or that I wasn't being looked after right now. But then how would I know when my people came home?

The other alternative was waiting in the back garden at number 11, so I'd be right there the moment Jay and the others arrived home. But there was nothing to eat there – I'd spent all of last night looking, and turned up nothing. Even the most seasoned hunter wouldn't have found a gingerbread man to catch in *that* garden.

So, stay and wait for my family but starve, or go and hope to find food but risk being alone forever?

This was not a good choice for a dog to have.

I stared across the road at Holly's house again. Obviously I couldn't risk sneaking in there again now, especially not while Mrs Templeton was also in residence. But maybe tonight, once Holly was in bed, I might be able to pop through the cat flap for some food? As long as Perdita didn't give me away.

Oh, who was I kidding? Perdita would be first in the line to send me to the pound.

My gaze travelled to the house next door. Kathleen. The house where I had first tasted gingerbread. Was that really only yesterday? It felt like an age already. And even longer since I'd last eaten.

Kathleen had been kind. Maybe she would let me in again.

It might be my last chance. If I couldn't get into Kathleen's house and eat a piece of gingerbread by the time the sun went down, then I'd leave Maple Drive and seek my fortune elsewhere.

I bobbed my head and, decision made, trotted across the road to number 10, where I sat and stared up at the door.

The problem with paws, of course, is that they're not made

for knocking. I could bark, or whine, I supposed, but that might draw undue attention from Holly next door. I didn't even know if Kathleen was inside, or if she'd gone out.

Suddenly, I heard footsteps behind me, and jumped round to check. Jack! He was still on the pavement, and hadn't spotted me yet, so I dived into the bush under the windowsill at the front of Kathleen's house. There, nestled in the relative warmth of the leaves and soil, I hid and watched Jack as he approached Holly's front door.

One more traitor in my midst. I couldn't risk running and being seen – plus there was no chance of getting gingerbread from Kathleen if I left now.

I huffed a sign, and hunkered down, resting my snout on my paws.

Seemed there was nothing to do but wait until Kathleen opened her door.

My eyes started to close, itching with tiredness after my restless night in the back garden. Maybe I could risk just a little snooze, before I made a final decision about my destiny.

DAISY

The buzzing sound that had drawn her out of sleep wouldn't go away. Daisy blinked in the dark of the bedroom, hemmed in by the heavy curtains around the bed, and finally realised what the noise was.

Her phone.

The ferry!

Fumbling to find the buzzing device on her bedside table, Daisy whacked Oliver on the shoulder until he woke up too. If they were calling to say they had space on the last ferry home, they'd need to get a move on – and quick! The bedside clock told her it was already 6.30. So, 5.30 UK time. And it felt it. Thank God the twins had decided to sleep in, for once.

'Hello?' she said, her voice scratchy. 'I mean, *bonjour*?'

'Mrs McCawley.' Daisy's spirits sank. She knew that voice. She recognised it from the information desk at the ferry. Henri. 'This is just a courtesy call to let you know that unfortunately no spaces have become available for you on this morning's ferry. We do hope that you will travel with us another time, and if we can be of any assistance—'

'You called me, at six thirty in the morning, to tell me I *can't* travel home today?' she ground out. Surely the man had a personal vendetta.

'Company policy is to call *all* passengers on our waiting lists. Successful or not.' The man's smarmy voice made Daisy's skin crawl. 'Now, would you like me to assist you in booking passage on another occasion? I could put you through to our bookings line ...'

'No,' Daisy snapped. 'You can't. Because it's six thirty in the morning on Christmas Eve and I don't believe for a moment that they're open. You're just *trying* to make my life miserable.'

Suddenly, the bedroom door flew open. 'Mum! Claude's gone viral!'

'What?!' Viral sounded bad. Daisy's brain immediately leapt to Mrs Templeton's comments about rabies, until she noticed that Bella was grinning. Her exhausted brain finally caught up. Viral was *good*. Viral meant more people searching for Claude. She covered the end of her phone with her hand. 'What's happening?'

'I assure you, madam, I am just doing my job,' Henri said, smugly. Daisy ignored him.

'The Find Claude campaign is all over social media,' Bella said, bouncing onto the bottom of the four poster bed with excitement. 'I mean *everywhere*! There's even a piece about him on the BBC website! And people are putting up posters, organising search parties ...'

'That's incredible!' Bella's excitement was infectious, and Daisy found herself grinning back at her daughter and forgetting all about the phone in her hand. At least, until Henri started talking again.

'Now, about your future travel home—'

'I don't know,' Daisy said, cutting him off with a sudden confidence she hadn't felt in years. 'I don't know how we're going to get home. But I can tell you one thing – we will. We are going to get home, find Claude and spend our Christmas together as a family.'

'And will you be doing this via our company?' Henri asked, apparently unaffected by the warrior spirit that had filled Daisy, as she sat bolt upright in bed.

'No, Henri. It will *not* be with your poxy ferry company. There are other ferries. Other ports. Hell, we could even take the Channel Tunnel if we wanted—' She broke off, staring at Bella, and then at Oliver, who had just about managed to struggle into a seated position.

'We can take the tunnel,' she repeated, in a whisper. Bella's eyes widened, and she nodded furiously.

'Mrs McCawley?' Henri said. 'If I could just take a moment to—' Daisy hung up on him. She wasn't wasting another moment on an imbecile who didn't understand that dogs were family too.

She was going home.

'The Channel Tunnel?' Oliver asked, his voice heavy with sleep. 'Is it open today? The car shuttle service, I mean?'

Sometimes, you didn't need to plan ahead. Sometimes, you didn't need to be super mum, with checklists and calendars and brilliant time-keeping skills.

Sometimes, you just had to follow your intuition, wherever it led you.

Daisy grinned. 'Let's drive to Calais and find out.'

JACK

The icicles were still missing, Jack realised, as he approached Holly's front door. It made the house feel bare, like every other house on the street. As if all of Holly's personality had been stripped from the place.

He missed the icicles. Hadn't she said she was going to put them back up? He wondered what had changed.

Glancing back over his shoulder as he waited for Holly to answer his knock, Jack spotted a piece of paper fluttering against the lamppost. With a frown, he moved closer to check it out.

FIND CLAUDE! The headline shouted. Underneath was a photo of a very familiar black and white dog, wearing a Santa between his bat-like ears. Apparently they weren't the only ones searching for him. Jack clocked the social media page link at the bottom of the poster. He'd have to check that out.

But then the door opened behind him, and he turned back to find Holly in the open doorway.

'You're here!' Holly cried, her eyes bright and her cheeks flushed. Was she baking again? Or drinking mulled wine without him? 'You won't believe what we've found!'

She dashed back through the hallway, leaving Jack on the doorstep.

'We?' he wondered, aloud, as he followed her inside, pulling the door shut behind him. 'Who is we?'

He got his answer as he stepped into the kitchen. Mrs Templeton sat at the head of the table, and Jack blinked at the strange sight. Was this another Christmas light intervention? Except Holly had seemed excited, not upset.

The end of the kitchen table had been cleared of all Holly's craft and baking supplies, presumably to make space for the tin that sat in their place.

'Mrs Templeton,' Jack said, politely. 'Lovely to see you.'

The older woman scowled up at him. Jack was oddly relieved at the evidence that not everything had changed.

'What's going on?' he asked.

'That blasted dog of yours—' Mrs Templeton started, but Holly spoke over her.

'I spotted Claude this morning,' she explained. 'He was digging in the school field.'

Jack glanced around the kitchen, his heart suddenly feeling too big in his chest. 'You found him? Where is he?'

Holly gave an apologetic smile. 'I'm sorry. He ran off again before I could get to him. But he looked fine, at least. All that gingerbread seems to be keeping him going. I've decorated my gingerbread house ready for when he comes home, too.'

'That's good.' Not as good as bringing him home would have been, but at least they knew now that Claude was still on Maple Drive, and he was okay. That was something. 'What was he doing on the school field?' he asked, with a frown. As far as he knew, there was no gingerbread there, and that seemed to be the only thing Claude was really interested in.

'He was digging for this,' Mrs Templeton said, picking up the tin. She held it, almost reverentially, out to Jack, who took it with trepidation.

'What is it?' he asked, even as his mind was running through the possibilities. *Bomb? No, this isn't Afghanistan. And it's a snowman themed tin. Probably not a bomb.*

'It's a time capsule,' Holly explained, and Jack looked at the tin with new interest. 'Mrs Templeton put it together with her students twenty-five years ago, when she was the headmistress at Forest Green.'

Mrs Templeton had been a headmistress? Well, that explained the general aura of fear she projected.

'And we're going to open it?' he asked.

Mrs Templeton scowled again. 'What do you think we've been trying to do? The hinges are rusted shut.'

'Do you want me to try?' Jack asked, already trying to work the lid off.

'I think this is going to take more than muscles,' Holly said, and Jack had to admit privately that she might be right. He probably *could* rip the lid off if he tried, but not without the risk of throwing the contents across the room. 'Hang on, I think I've got what we need.' She disappeared out into the hallway, and Jack heard her opening the under stairs cupboard.

'So, what's in the time capsule?' Jack figured he might as well *try* to make small talk with Holly's ornery neighbour.

She gave him a scornful look. 'It was twenty-five years ago. Do you really think I'd remember the details now?'

'I suppose not.' Some days, it was hard to remember what he'd eaten for breakfast. Yet the memory of Claude's head nestled against his lap remained strong.

'Besides, it was a secret capsule. Everyone had to put a note about their Christmas memories or dreams inside an envelope, along with something that made them think of Christmas. No one saw each other's. We were supposed to open it ten years later, but then … well, a new headmistress took over, and I suppose I might have forgotten to mention it to her.'

A new headmistress. Jack rather got the impression that Mrs Templeton's leaving Forest Green School might not have been entirely voluntary. Maybe that explained why she was so bitter all the time. Fifteen years resenting being pushed out could do that to a person, he supposed.

'So *nobody* knows everything that's inside this capsule,' Jack said. 'That's exciting.'

'I wonder, sometimes, where all the children are now that contributed to it,' Mrs Templeton said, sounding very far away. Then she shook her head. 'But of course, they've all grown up, moved on. Moved away, mostly, I imagine. Certainly, none of them ever came back to find it.'

'I suppose they might have forgotten,' Jack said.

'Or they didn't care enough in the first place,' Mrs Templeton snapped. 'I poured my life into that school, into those pupils, but in the end … well. Anyway.'

'Anyway,' Jack echoed, not really sure what else to say.

Thankfully, Holly reappeared to break the moment.

'This should do it!' She held aloft some sort of craft device that looked mostly like a pair of angled pliers, but with bright pink and flowery handles. 'Hand it over?'

The floral device worked. Holly levered open the lid carefully, with a ping as the rusted hinges finally gave way. The tin was deep, and bigger than the usual sort of biscuit tin Jack was used to.

'Wow!' Holly said, peering in. 'There are a lot of envelopes in here! And also something …' she sniffed. 'What's that smell?'

'I imagine, whatever attracted Claude to it in the first place,' Jack guessed. Something, whatever it was, had held its strong, cinnamon and ginger scent for more than two decades. He dreaded to think how much it must have stank when it was first put in the capsule.

'Let me see.' Mrs Templeton shoved Holly impatiently out of the way, and reached inside the box to grab the top envelope. Ripping it open, she pulled out a small, wooden decoration, and a scrap of lined notepaper. Unfolding it, she read it, then placed it on the table beside the box.

Rolling her eyes at Jack, Holly picked it up and read the note aloud. '"My Christmas Memory, by Caitlin Manners. My favourite Christmas memory is singing in the carol service at school, with all my friends."' She put the paper back and smiled. 'Aw, that's nice. I always loved my school carol service, too.'

'We used to walk through the town to the church,' Mrs Templeton said absently, her hands already busy opening the next envelope. 'A whole parade of children, all in perfectly pressed ties and shirts, ready to sing for the whole community.'

'It sounds lovely,' Jack said. Somehow, Mrs Templeton managed to make it sound like an indictment on modern society that this no longer happened, just through her tone. It was, he decided, a very special talent – even if it wasn't one anyone else appreciated very much.

'It was more than nice. It was a community service.' Her eyes scanned the next note, and she placed it on top of the first one.

This time, Jack picked it up. '"My favourite thing about Christmas is the presents. By Robbie Jacobs." Well, nice to know some things don't change.'

Mrs Templeton shot him a glare. 'Robbie Jacobs' family never had two pennies to rub together. At Christmas, we at the school would make sure he had something to open on Christmas morning. It was probably the only time he had anything new all year.'

She went back to opening envelopes, and Jack exchanged a look with Holly. Apparently Mrs Templeton had hidden depths of compassion. Very hidden. And very, very deep. But they were there.

What had happened to change her into the bitter old woman they knew today? Was it losing her job at the school? Or was it something more?

'This community used to be like that, you know,' Mrs Templeton went on, smoothing out the next note and adding to the pile, and standing up a little model of a reindeer on the table in front of her. 'We looked out for each other. Took care of those who needed it. It used to be a *real* community. But it seems like I'm the only one who remembers that.'

'That's a lovely thing to do,' Holly said, looking touched.

Mrs Templeton didn't reply, too engrossed in the next note in the box. Her hands shook as she placed it on the pile, and Jack frowned as he reached for it.

'"My Christmas wish is that the whole community come together to celebrate Christmas this year, and every year. By …"' He paused, and Holly looked up at him. '"By Mrs E B Templeton,"' he finished.

Holly's mouth opened just a little as she stared at Jack. Jack met her gaze as they both searched for what to say next.

In the end, Mrs Templeton beat them to it.

'I always thought that Maple Drive could be more than it is,' she said, her tone misty and far away. 'Yes, we'd lend a hand and work together, but at the end of the day everyone went home to their own houses, and that was it. I always wanted it to be … closer, somehow. A true community, sharing and celebrating together.'

And unfortunately, she tended to try to force that collaboration by issuing draconian orders about Christmas decorations. *Not* the best way to foster community spirit, in Jack's opinion.

Holly, meanwhile, seemed more forgiving.

Sliding into the seat beside Mrs Templeton, she said, 'It sounds wonderful. That's exactly what I was looking for when I moved here, you know. And when I took the job at Forest Green. A community I could belong to.' She looked up at Jack, and made a small motion with her head.

Was she asking him to do something? Probably. But what? Hand signals in combat situations he could follow no problem. Hints from a woman ... they were a million times trickier.

'I know Jack was too,' Holly added, her voice heavy with meaning, and Jack caught on at last.

'That's right.' He took the seat on the other side of Mrs Templeton. 'When I left the army, I was hoping to find a new family, a new community, out here in civilian life.'

For a moment Mrs Templeton softened, her expression sympathetic. 'You saw it too. The potential.'

'We did,' Holly said.

But then Mrs Templeton's mouth tightened into a straight line again, and she shook her head as if to dispel any weakness. 'Still, you both came to the wrong place. Everything I wished for, it never happened.'

'But you still wish it would, don't you?' Holly placed a hand over Mrs Templeton's and, to Jack's surprise, the older woman didn't push it away.

'It was twenty-five years ago,' Mrs Templeton snapped, but there was less venom in it now. Jack almost thought he heard an actual wobble in her voice.

'Still. It *could* happen. It is the season of miracles, after all.' Holly's gaze fixed onto Jack's as she spoke. What was she thinking? He wished he knew.

Then Holly jerked her head towards the huge Christmas cake propped up on the dresser in the corner of the kitchen, and an envelope with Kathleen's name printed neatly on the front, and suddenly he got it.

Jack couldn't help but grin as he realised what Holly had planned. She really was something special.

'We realised last night that Kathleen, next door, is going to be on her own for Christmas,' he said, and Holly gave him a small smile. 'We thought we might do something to celebrate with her, since Holly and I are both alone for the day this year too. Perhaps you might like to join us?' he suggested.

'It's not the whole community, I know, but it might be a start,' Holly added. 'And maybe there are others who are alone this Christmas who would want to join us.'

'I won't be alone. My son and his family will be here,' Mrs Templeton said quickly. Somehow, it didn't sound like an outright no. 'Apparently they won't be staying long this year, though. So I *might* have some time to help you out.'

Spending Christmas Day with Mrs Templeton wasn't his idea of a good time, but he couldn't very well talk about wanting to find a community and then let a neighbour spend half the day alone, when he could help.

Perhaps, Jack realised, as Mrs Templeton's face creaked up into something resembling a smile, it wasn't about finding a community at all.

Perhaps it was about building one.

And maybe this, right here, could be the first step.

CHAPTER
TWELVE

CLAUDE

When I woke up from my small nap in the hedge under Kathleen's window, the sun was already on its way down again. Days are so short in the winter, sometimes it was a struggle to fit all my meals into the daylight hours.

That hadn't been a problem today, though. My rumbling stomach woke me up. Again!

Really, this was unacceptable.

Well, I'd made myself a promise. Either I'd get that gingerbread by nightfall, or I'd leave Maple Drive.

It was make or break time.

Kathleen still showed no sign of opening the front door, so I figured I was going to have to find another way in. Checking around to ensure that I wasn't being watched – and that neither Holly nor Jack had slipped out of number 12 when I wasn't looking – I bent my little legs and jumped, straining my neck to see through Kathleen's window.

No good. All I could see were the leaves left on the bush I'd been napping in.

I shuffled back a little way, out of the bush, and tried again, springing up like a bird about to take flight, my paws scrabbling at air as I stretched out to try and make it to the window.

Still nothing. The closest I got was the bricks under the windowsill.

I sighed, and scooted back a little further. I couldn't give up now. If Kathleen could just see me, I reasoned, she'd have to come and let me in. I just had to alert her to my presence.

Which meant more jumping.

This time, when my nose barely made it to windowsill height, I didn't pause. I surged straight back up again, launching myself higher and higher with each jump. I was going to make it! I was! I could almost *taste* that gingerbread!

My nose edged above the windowsill, and this time I could see inside, just for a second. Long enough to see Kathleen, sitting on her sofa. I jumped again, trying to get her attention – would she hear me bark through the window? I wasn't sure.

With each jump, I saw a little more – Kathleen, a book in her lap. No, not a book. An album, filled with pictures, like the ones Daisy had of Bella and Jay. Another jump. Was she … was she crying? I couldn't tell.

I wanted to comfort her. To sit with her and let her pet my head. And feed me gingerbread.

Just one more jump …

'What on *earth* are you doing?' Perdita's lazy purr of a question coming from behind me disrupted my balance, and I landed awkwardly, scrabbling to try and find my balance and stay upright.

I huffed round in a circle to face her. 'None of your business.' This wasn't her house, and these weren't her gingerbread men.

'When you're making such an idiot of yourself right next door to *my* house, then it's my business,' Perdita replied, in between licking her paws.

They probably had food on them. For a brief, insane

second, I considered trying to lick her paws myself.

Then I came to my senses and realised she'd scratch my eyes out in a heartbeat.

'Look, you *have* a home to go to tonight,' I pointed out. 'One with food and warm radiators and nice humans. Why don't you just go to it and *leave me alone*?'

Perdita sat back on her hind legs and surveyed me with her cool, green gaze. 'And here I was thinking you might be looking for a bed for the night.'

'Gingerbread, actually.' The sky was getting darker by the moment. Soon, I'd have to admit defeat, and leave Maple Drive forever.

It made my heart hurt just thinking about it.

Perdita's nose wrinkled up. 'Gingerbread? Really? What's wrong with a nice piece of salmon?'

I shuddered. Fish is not my thing.

'Well, if that's what you really want, I suppose Holly will have some of that, too. In fact, I think she has a whole *house* made of it, actually.' Perdita turned, her long, bushy tail swishing behind her as she sashayed down the path. Then she looked back over her shoulder. 'Well? Are you coming?'

'With … you?' I asked, confused.

Perdita huffed impatiently. 'Of course, with me. It's Christmas Eve, Claude. Whatever our differences, I'm not going to leave you out here to freeze on Christmas Eve.'

'Why not?' Because, quite honestly, that was *exactly* the sort of thing I expected Perdita to do. She was my nemesis cat, after all.

She didn't look at me as she replied. 'Holly wouldn't like it.'

Aha! That made sense. For all her airs and graces and independence, Perdita was just as afraid of disappointing her human as the rest of us were.

It almost made her more dog-like to me.

But I couldn't accept.

'I can't,' I said, hating the words even as I said them. 'Holly and Jack – and Mrs Templeton. They'll call the pound if they see me again. I heard them say so.'

'So don't let them see you,' Perdita advised. 'At least, not until tomorrow. I heard Holly saying how *everywhere* is shut tomorrow for Christmas Day. I think it's a safe bet that includes the pound, don't you?'

Hope began to fill my chest. 'But how will I get inside without being seen?' I asked, praying Perdita had an answer for this, the way she always had an answer for everything. I might even listen, this time.

'The humans are all busy with some box full of rubbish,' Perdita said, dismissively. 'I'll go in first, make sure they're all distracted. Then you can sneak in behind me. We'll hide you in the spare room until later tonight.'

It sounded like a reasonable plan, I supposed. There was just one thing …

'Is there any food in the spare room?'

DAISY

'I'm just saying, maybe we should call before we drive all the way to Calais,' Oliver said, as Daisy loaded the cases into the car.

'Absolutely,' she agreed, turning back to grab the next lot of bags. 'You call. But we're going to Calais regardless.'

'Right. And ... why is that exactly?'

Daisy sighed, and turned to face her husband. Inside the chateau, she could hear her mother chatting to the twins in baby talk, and Jay racing around with Petal. Her dad, meanwhile, was trying to fix the oven, again, while fending off the birds that had taken to swooping over his head.

'Because we can't stay here,' she said, bluntly. 'The place is falling down, my parents are completely out of their depth, and we need to get home to Claude. Calais is one step closer to home, and gives us options.'

'If we can get on the train,' Oliver pointed out.

'And even if we can't,' Daisy countered. 'We can book into a hotel for the night, or even try the other ferry companies. Maybe one of them runs later on Christmas Eve. But I bet there are a lot more trains going than ferries today – and tomorrow, for that matter. Remember? We looked at it when we were booking the ferry, but *you* thought travelling by boat was more of an adventure, for some reason.' God damn her

217

husband and his *Swallows and Amazons* fantasies.

'Boats are always an adventure.'

'They are also not an option right now. So, Calais.'

'So I should call the tunnel people?' Oliver asked, his brow creased up.

'Yes. That would be a good idea.' Daisy slammed the boot shut on the world's most well-travelled M&S hamper. Hopefully that was everything, bar the children. Because she sure as hell wasn't coming back for anything they'd forgotten this time. 'But first, get everyone in the car. Because we are going to Calais!'

They travelled in convoy; Daisy driving, Oliver navigating while also making phone calls to try to arrange their return travel, and Bella following in the car behind with her grandparents. Every time Daisy checked her rear-view mirror, she'd see her dad giving her a thumbs up, and sigh. It was going to be a long journey.

'Okay, so there's no space on today's trains at the moment,' Oliver said. 'But they are running tomorrow morning.'

'You know, before today, I'd have wondered who on earth wants to travel across the Channel on Christmas Day,' Daisy mused, signalling to turn left and checking her mirror to make sure her father had done the same. 'But now I know.'

'People who can't bear to spend their Christmases in France?' Oliver asked.

'People desperate to spend Christmas with their loved ones, no matter what,' Daisy corrected him.

It might take them a little longer than anticipated, but they would be back in Maple Drive in time to give Claude his bone patterned Christmas stocking full of treats, one way or another.

'Do you want me to book spaces for tomorrow, then?' Oliver asked.

Daisy shook her head. 'Keep trying. I want to get back today if we can. If we can't ... well, we'll look at travelling on Christmas Day as a last resort.'

It took them just over five hours to reach Calais, including bathroom breaks for Jay and nappy changes for the twins, and the half hour pause when Daisy's mother spotted an antiques emporium that might have 'just the perfect thing for the front bedroom!'

'We're going to spend the whole of the next year trying to persuade them to move home in time for Christmas, aren't we?' Oliver muttered, as they waited outside with the buggy.

'That or a hell of a lot of DIY,' Daisy agreed.

But that was a problem for next year. First, they had to get home for Christmas.

By the time they arrived in Calais, Oliver had called the ticket line eight times, and got the same answer to each call: there were no spaces left on today's trains, but they might be able to fit them on tomorrow, still. 'Shall I book it now?' Oliver asked.

'Not yet,' Daisy replied.

Oliver sighed. 'So, what do we do now, then?'

Daisy flashed him a smile. 'It's time to find out if there's any room at the inn.'

'Wait,' Bella said, when they parked up to discuss the plan with her grandparents. 'You cannot seriously be planning on walking around Calais on Christmas Eve, knocking on doors, until we find a hotel with enough space to take all of us.'

'It was good enough for Mary and Joseph,' Grandad said, sounding rather like he was relishing the challenge. Or perhaps just grateful to have escaped his bird-infested chateau.

'Mary and Joseph didn't have the internet,' Bella pointed out. 'We do.' She grabbed Jay's tablet from him with a sigh and, overriding the parental controls Daisy had put in place, brought up a hotel comparison website. 'Right. What are we looking for?'

'Um, three rooms?' Daisy said. 'One double with space for the twins' travel cots, a twin room for you and Jay next door, preferably, and another double for Granny and Grandad.'

Bella typed some things into the tablet. 'On it. I'll check in on the Find Claude campaign, too. Last I heard, someone had spotted Claude jumping up and down in one of the gardens on Maple Drive, but by the time they got there, he was gone.'

'At least we know he's still on Maple Drive,' Daisy said. 'And we'll be home soon.' She hoped.

Bella glanced up. 'You guys might as well find us some lunch. I'll have us somewhere to stay by the time you get back.'

Daisy and Oliver exchanged a look. When had their daughter grown so capable? So in control?

'Okay, then,' Oliver said.

'Wait!' Bella called, as they turned to go. Daisy looked back to see her daughter's best innocent smile. 'Leave me your credit card?'

JACK

'So, what do we do now?' Holly asked, as Mrs Templeton tottered down the pathway back towards her own house, with promises of pigs in blankets and eggnog for the next day. 'And, do you mind? About Mrs Templeton, I mean?'

Jack shook his head, watched Mrs Templeton open her front door then shut it behind her, and turned back to face Holly with a smile. 'It's fine,' he said, shutting her front door, too. 'You were right. We couldn't just leave her to spend Christmas on her own, if her family aren't planning on sticking around. Not when we're organising something especially so that neither of us nor Kathleen are alone.'

Holly tilted her head as she looked at him. 'You realise I never actually said any of that, right?'

Jack blinked. 'But you were thinking it. Weren't you?'

'I was.'

'I guess I must have read your mind, then.'

Holly's smile spread wide across her face, her lips pink and soft in the light from the Christmas tree fairy lights. 'That's quite the talent you have there.'

'I'm a talented man.'

'I'm sure you are.'

Were they flirting again? Jack was pretty damn sure that

was what was going on, but he'd already learned that he couldn't make too many assumptions when it came to Holly, mind reading notwithstanding. And he couldn't forget that he might be leaving soon.

He shook his head, and followed Holly back into the kitchen. Those were questions for another day. Another year, even, maybe. First they had to get through Christmas with Kathleen and Mrs Templeton.

And they had to find Claude.

Suddenly, Jack remembered the Find Claude poster outside.

'Hey, do you have your laptop or tablet handy?' he asked.

'Sure. Why?' Holly reached over to the counter, where a pile of Christmas crafts had been stacked, and grabbed her tablet from its precarious position on the top of the pile.

'There's a poster on the lamppost outside,' Jack explained, as she unlocked the screen and handed it over to him. 'Part of the campaign to find Claude that the McCawleys' daughter set up, I think. I never thought to check it out last night, but if they've got as far as posters ...'

'It's worth a look,' Holly finished for him, taking the seat beside him and looking over his shoulder. 'Wow!'

'Yeah.' Jack scrolled through the screen, past hundreds of messages of support – and a link to the BBC website and their report on Claude. 'I just figured it was a thing with her school friends, but it looks like it grew!'

'Any news from the McCawleys?' Holly asked.

Jack scanned the page. 'They're still trying to get back. Apparently they're in Calais right now, trying to get a place on the car train.'

'Then they could be home really soon. That's good. I'm sure Claude will come out of hiding once they're here.'

'Yeah.' Jack handed the tablet back. Soon, Claude would be the McCawleys' problem again, not his. He just wished he'd been able to find him for them. Keep him safe and well fed on gingerbread.

'So, you never answered my question,' Holly said, topping up their wine glasses. They'd moved past mulled wine now, and onto the real stuff, which Jack was grateful for. All those spices had given him a headache – not that he'd ever admit that to Holly. 'And since I can't read *your* mind I'm going to have to ask it again. What do we do now?'

Suddenly, in a flash, Jack knew what he wanted to do, the image so firmly printed on his brain it felt like a memory, rather than a fantasy. He wanted to curl up on the sofa with Holly in his arms, Claude at his feet, and watch bad Christmas telly before scooping Holly up and carrying her to bed. And then he wanted to—

Well. It didn't matter. Because a fantasy was all it was. And that wasn't what Holly even meant by her question, he suspected.

'You mean, about Kathleen's Christmas surprise?' he guessed, trying to shake off the image of him and Holly, headed to bed together on Christmas Eve.

'Yeah. I mean, we got so caught up with Mrs Templeton's time capsule, we've barely started. And it's not like we had a detailed plan to start with.'

Holly, Jack suspected, liked a plan. Which suited him just fine. In his experience, plans quite often fell apart at the first hurdle, but trying to get anything started without one was a recipe for disaster in itself.

'Well, let's think. We want to give her a proper Christmas, right?'

'And ourselves, too,' Holly added, with a small smile. 'I

mean, it's for all four of us, right? So that none of us has to spend Christmas alone.'

'Good point,' Jack conceded. It was about all of them. And right now, in the moment, he wanted it to be perfect for Holly. Never mind the others. If he could give this lovely, lonely woman a perfect Christmas, he'd feel he'd done his duty at Maple Drive. Maybe then he could move on, with no regrets.

Or maybe, just maybe, he might even find a reason to stay.

'So, where would you start, if you were putting together your perfect Christmas?' he asked.

Holly tilted her head again, considering, and Jack took a moment to appreciate the long, white line of her neck, and the sparkly pins that held her wavy blonde hair away from her face. She was so beautiful, it was hard to imagine any man walking away from her willingly.

Clearly her ex was an idiot.

And right then, watching her dream up her perfect Christmas, Jack decided that he wouldn't be an idiot too. If Holly gave him an indication that she wanted him to hang around Maple Drive a little longer, well, he'd do it. If there was a chance that Holly could be more than just Christmas for him, if there was even the smallest possibility that she could be the future and the family he was looking for, he had to take it.

If it didn't work out, then he could move on later. There were always other places, other jobs, other streets. He had nothing else tying him to Maple Drive.

But his boss had been right. He couldn't give up before he gave Maple Drive – and Holly – a proper chance.

'Decorations,' Holly said, at last, answering the question Jack had almost forgotten he's asked. 'I'd start with decorations.'

Kathleen, Christmas, planning ... that was what they were

talking about. Not the possibility of romance.

Jack hauled his errant brain back to the conversation at hand. 'Well, your house is looking pretty thoroughly decorated. And I'm not sure how we'd get into Kathleen's house to decorate without her noticing. So maybe we should move down the list.'

But Holly shook her head. 'We might not be able to decorate *inside* her house …' she said, leaving it dangling for him to catch on.

'Icicles,' he said, remembering the lights she'd taken down from the outside of the house. 'Of course.'

'Oh, I've got much more than just icicles here.' Holly placed a hand on a large stack of delivery boxes beside her. What was in them? And, more to the point, why hadn't *he* delivered them? 'Special delivery one-day courier service from my favourite online Christmas decoration store,' Holly explained. 'I've got enough here to light up the entire street.'

'Mrs Templeton will have a heart attack,' Jack pointed out.

'I don't know,' Holly replied, thoughtfully. 'I mean, she seemed almost human, looking through the time capsule this afternoon. And besides, her big problem with my lights was that no one else in the street had any up, so they stood out.'

'But if everyone has lights up …' Well, then the whole street would look a hell of a lot more festive. And the huge smile on Holly's face told him that it would be worth it.

Apparently, he was spending his Christmas Eve decorating Maple Drive. Strangely, he didn't mind one bit.

And if Claude was still out there on Maple Drive, putting up lights might help them find him.

CHAPTER
THIRTEEN

CLAUDE

'It's all clear,' Perdita whispered through the cat flap. 'They're doing something with boxes.'

I gave her a second to stand back, then launched myself at the cat flap. Apparently, the lack of food I'd consumed in the last day or so – since my last, lovely piece of gingerbread – had streamlined my impressive physique. I slipped through the cat flap a lot easier than I had the day before, anyway.

Holly's kitchen was lit up from within, with strings of lights of every colour spread out across the kitchen table, and into the hallway. I could hear Jack and Holly talking in the other room, and glanced between the sound source and Perdita's food bowl. Priorities, priorities. Food, or avoiding the pound?

Put like that, it was simple.

I dived for the food bowl, wolfing down as much cat food as I could stand in the shortest amount of time, then spun back round to Perdita. 'So, where do I hide?'

Perdita narrowed her eyes. 'Nowhere. Not until you've got rid of all the food around your mouth. I'm not having you make a mess of my lovely home.'

Impatiently, I ran my tongue around my face, savouring the last few morsels. 'Happy?'

'Barely.' Perdita stalked towards the kitchen door. 'Come on.'

I followed, cautiously, but Jack and Holly seemed far more engrossed in their strings of lights than anything else going on this evening. That was good. I hoped Perdita was right, and that the pound would be closed tomorrow. It was early evening now; maybe it was closed already.

But maybe I'd stay out of sight for a *little* bit longer, just in case.

'This way,' Perdita hissed, the 's' on 'this' stretched out. She was already half way up the stairs.

Hopping over a string of lights shaped like snowflakes, I made it to the stairs and scurried up them behind her.

Perdita led me to a small room at the front of the house, with a single bed and a small desk under the window. 'She never uses this room,' she said, treading lightly on the bed spread. 'You'll be safe here.'

Downstairs, I heard doors opening and closing again, and Jack and Holly laughing as they left the house. Where were they going? Jumping up onto the desk, I peered out into the growing darkness, watching them leave. Jack had two large boxes in his arms, and Holly had another. They crossed the road, and knocked on the door at number 9.

'So, what are you going to do now?' Perdita asked, and I hopped down back onto the bed. It felt strange to be here, taking refuge with my enemy. But I was grateful to have a roof over my head tonight.

'I thought I might nap,' I said, considering my options. 'Unless you know the whereabouts of that gingerbread house …?' I added, hopefully.

'I meant about your family,' Perdita said, sitting back on her hind paws again, her tail wrapped around her fluffy body. 'If they come back. What will you do?'

'*When* they come back,' I corrected. 'They're definitely coming back.'

'They haven't so far.'

'They had somewhere to be. They were visiting Granny and Grandad.' At least, that's what I hoped. France, ferry and chateau still sounded a little too strange and exotic for me. 'As soon as they're done they'll come back, and everything will be back to normal.' That's what I had to keep clinging on to.

'Will it?' Perdita asked. 'They abandoned you, Claude. They left you here alone with no food, and nowhere to sleep. If it wasn't for me you'd still be out there in the cold.'

'They didn't mean to. They put me in my crate, I just jumped out … to chase you, actually. This is really all your fault, you know.'

Perdita pressed her front paws against the bed cover, and I heard her claws pulling at the threads every time she lifted them. 'At least I noticed you were still here. At least I'm helping you now. I'm here. They're not.'

'They'll be back,' I said again. 'And then we can get back to normal.' But even as I said the words, I realised what Perdita was getting at. How could things be normal again, after this? Whether they meant to or not, my people had left me alone – and they hadn't come back. I could understand not realising I wasn't in the car.

But I couldn't get past the idea that they hadn't come back for me.

What did that mean?

'Now you're getting it,' Perdita said, watching me carefully. 'You know, I can almost see the thoughts going through your head. You're realising that they didn't care about you enough to come back, aren't you? So, I'll ask you again, what are you going to do next?'

'I don't know,' I said, slowly, staring past her at an empty space on the wall. What would I do? They were still my people, even if they'd let me down. But if I couldn't trust them to take care of me … maybe I *would* be better at the pound, with a chance of finding a family who could love me the way I'd love them.

Or maybe I should have left Maple Drive as I'd planned. Maybe the family I'd always taken for granted wasn't mine, after all.

Perhaps it was time to find a new one.

'I'll see if I can find you some gingerbread,' Perdita said, with more sympathy than I expected from her. 'You look like you need it.'

'Thanks.' I watched her go, her padding paws silent on the carpet, then hunkered down on the bed, my head on my paws, my mind full of whirring thoughts and feelings I wasn't used to.

It used to be so simple. Love your people, get loved in return. That was the way it was meant to be.

When had it grown so complicated?

Perdita was right. Everything would be a lot easier with gingerbread.

'Here you go.' Perdita slunk through the door, a piece of gingerbread in the shape of a snowman in her mouth, and deposited it on the floor. I jumped down and devoured it a couple of quick bites, then looked up at Perdita hopefully. She rolled her eyes. 'There's more downstairs, and Jack and Holly are still out. You can fetch your own this time.'

Suddenly, the room lit up with a flash of pink and yellow lights from outside the window.

'What was that?' Perdita prowled past me and jumped up onto the windowsill to look. I followed, clambering back up onto the bed then leaping across the inches to the desk, and stared out of the window in amazement.

Two of the houses in Maple Drive were lit up like Holly's Christmas tree in the hallway – all bright colours and flashing lights, making out patterns and pictures on the walls of the houses. In the street, I could just make out Holly and Jack crossing the road and knocking on another door. Were they doing this? Why?

'Come on,' Perdita said. 'I want to find out what's going on out there.'

I hesitated. I was interested too. But Perdita had said there was more gingerbread downstairs …

'We can grab the gingerbread on our way out,' she added, and I jumped down from the desk to follow her.

DAISY

By the time that evening fell, Daisy, Oliver, the kids and the grandparents were all happily ensconced in the small, family run hotel that Bella had found for them, close to the station. And that meant it was time for another phase of Daisy's constantly changing plans.

Once, just once, she'd like *something* to go right the first time, so they could actually stick with Plan A. Or even B or C.

The way they were going, she was running out of letters of the alphabet.

'So, do you know where we're going?' Oliver asked, as he and Daisy left the hotel.

'To the information desk at the Eurotunnel terminal,' Daisy said, absently, checking the cheaply printed, free map in her hands. Was she even holding it the right way up? She should have brought Bella. Bella was much better at directions than either of them. 'I figure, if we're there in person, they'll have to give us a space. Right?'

'That's the hope.' Oliver took the map from her, turned it the other way up, squinted at it, then turned it back the way she'd had it in the first place. 'Come on. I think it's this way.'

Daisy rolled her eyes, but followed.

In the end, getting tickets for the following day proved a

damn sight easier than trying to get home on Christmas Eve. Daisy had been holding out a small, faint hope that when they showed up in person, space on the Christmas Eve train would miraculously appear, and they'd dash back to fetch the family and cancel their hotel rooms, and be home with Claude before Santa made his rounds.

No such luck with that, though. But …

'At least we know we can get home tomorrow,' Oliver said, wrapping a reassuring arm around her shoulder as they left the ticket office. 'That's something, right?'

'I suppose.' But it meant leaving Claude alone for *another* night. Not to mention spending their Christmas Day travelling home from Calais via Folkestone. Not exactly the perfect Christmas she'd been hoping for.

Daisy sighed. At least they were all together, Claude notwithstanding. That had to be what mattered most.

'Come on,' she said, pulling the map from her pocket again. 'We need to get back to the kids, and rescue my parents.' And given the confusion with the map on the way there, they'd better get moving quickly, if they wanted to get back to the hotel before Jay needed putting to bed.

'Actually …' Oliver stopped walking, and reached out to take her hand.

'What?' Daisy asked, suspiciously. He had that look he got, whenever he'd had what he thought was a brilliant idea but turned out to be wildly inconvenient and annoying. Just what she didn't need on Christmas Eve.

'I spoke with your mum before we left. She and your dad are going to watch the kids for a couple of hours.'

'While we do what, exactly?' All she really wanted to do was fall face first in a bed and pass out until they were home again. But apparently that wasn't an option.

Oliver smiled. 'Come with me.'

Suppressing a frustrated sigh, Daisy let him lead her through the streets of Calais, too tired to take in the festive decorations, or even the holiday atmosphere.

'Do you remember the last time we came here?' he asked, and Daisy blinked as she remembered.

'Um, ten years ago? More? It was when Bella was small.'

'And before we'd even thought of Jay. Or the twins.'

Daisy allowed herself a small smile. God, they'd thought one kid was hard. Thought they desperately needed a break. And her parents had sympathised, taking Bella for a weekend so she and Oliver could escape to France for a romantic weekend. They'd had a night in Calais, a night out at some hotel a half hour or so away – out in the French countryside – that Oliver's colleague had been raving about, then caught the ferry home, the car loaded up with wine to repay her parents for the babysitting.

'I remember it being a lot easier to get in and out of France in those days,' Daisy said, drily, and Oliver laughed – a proper, head tipped back, belly laugh. Never mind Calais; when was the last time she'd heard that? She could hardly remember.

What had happened to them? When had the man she loved become more of an annoyance than a friend?

And how did she change that?

'Come on,' Oliver said, grabbing her hand again. 'This way.'

He led her down a small side street, and Daisy frowned a little as she looked around. It seemed familiar somehow. But really, it had been a decade, and she hadn't paid all that much attention to Calais's not-exactly-renowned attractions even then. She'd been far more interested in her husband.

But then Oliver took a sharp left turn, and the awnings of a familiar restaurant came into view, making Daisy stop still in the middle of the street.

'It's still here?' she whispered. To be honest, she'd seldom thought of the tiny restaurant where Oliver and she had whiled away a whole afternoon waiting for their hotel room to be ready, but now she saw it again, she couldn't believe it hadn't closed up or been passed on or at least changed in some way.

But when Oliver held the door open for her, everything looked exactly as she remembered. Same rickety wooden tables. Same faded linens. Same chalkboard above the bar area, detailing their limited menu. She thought she might even recognise some of the waiting staff.

Oliver hauled out his rusty French to ask for a table and, in no time, they were seated, bread basket between them and menus in hand.

'How did you know this place was still here?' Daisy asked, over the top of her menu, while a nearby waiter hovered obviously, waiting for their orders.

Oliver shrugged, his menu still folded on the table in front of him. 'I didn't. Just took a chance.'

'Do you remember what we talked about that afternoon we spent here?' Daisy asked.

'I think we talked about everything,' Oliver joked. 'Politics, religion, literature … Bella mostly, of course.'

'We talked about the future,' Daisy said, remembering. 'We talked about all the things we wanted from our future together.'

'You said four kids,' Oliver said. 'I totally blame you for the twins.'

Daisy laughed, and the waiter lost patience, approaching their table with an expectant look.

Oliver ordered the wine, because he cared more about it than she did, and Daisy ordered the special from the blackboard over the bar, while Oliver settled for a traditional *moules frites*.

When the waiter had left to pass on their requests, Oliver sat back in his chair and watched her, making Daisy fidget as she tucked her hair behind her ear.

'What?' she asked.

Oliver shook his head. 'Nothing, really. Just thinking about how beautiful you are. And how lucky I am to have you.'

Daisy smiled back. Maybe one evening alone wouldn't be enough to put right everything that had grown tired and ignored in their marriage. But it might be a really good start.

HOLLY

'A little more to the left!' Holly called up, shading her eyes against the brightness of the Christmas lights next door, as she directed Jack in the placement of Kathleen's decorations. They'd left hers until last so that, if she noticed and came out to see what was going on, the whole street would already be ablaze with festivity. Well, almost the whole street, anyway.

Holly was amazed at how many people in Maple Drive had been happy for them to hang lights on their houses, just for a couple of nights. She'd expected a lot of slammed doors in their faces. Instead, people had been surprisingly helpful.

'Any sign of Claude yet?' had been the number one thing people said upon answering the door to them.

Holly wouldn't have known how to go about answering, or asking for what they needed, but Jack had no qualms. With that easy smile that made her middle feel a little gooey, he'd said, 'Not yet. So if you see him, give me a yell – I'd hate to think of Claude all alone on Christmas Eve. But actually, there was something else we wanted to ask you this evening. It's about celebrating Christmas, here in Maple Drive. Tell me, do you know Holly, from number 12?'

Not everyone had been a fan of outdoor lights, but when they'd seen the selection Holly had to offer, almost everyone had managed to find *something* they liked. A few people had been concerned about Mrs Templeton – usually people who'd tried to put lights up in the past, only to have official complaints made to the council. But Jack had even managed to set their minds at ease.

'We spent the afternoon with Mrs Templeton, actually, looking through an old time capsule, from when she was headmistress at Forest Green. I think the main problem she had with the lights was that she wanted all the houses in Maple Drive to look the same, like a real, connected community. Don't you think, Holly?'

Holly had nodded sagely at that. 'Community is very important to Mrs Templeton.'

'So if all the houses have lights, I'm sure there won't be anything for her to object to.'

Then he'd flashed that smile again, and the householder had given in. Every time.

'Where did you learn to do that?' she'd asked, somewhere between numbers 9 and 7.

'Do what?' Jack had replied, his forehead creased in confusion.

And Holly had realised that it wasn't a trick, wasn't something he'd studied or learned. It was just who he was.

She smiled up as she watched him balancing on the top of the ladder, affixing a twinkly snowman to Kathleen's roof. Well, it would sparkle, once they had it plugged in. They were running it from Holly's outside socket for now, until Kathleen agreed that she wanted the lights up.

Holly glanced back across the road. The only houses that were still dark were numbers 11 and 13 – the McCawleys and Mrs Templeton. She wondered if the McCawleys would really mind if they just put up a few small lights … but she supposed Jack was right. They'd better wait until they came home.

And as for Mrs Templeton … well. They'd just have to see what she made of the rest of the street, first.

'Okay up there?' she called, and Jack nodded, the gesture barely visible in the darkness, despite the lights.

'Nearly there … Done.' He manoeuvred his body straight against the ladder again, and Holly let out a small sigh of relief. 'Want to plug us in before I come down? Just in case?'

'Will do.' Hopping across to her own garden, Holly flicked the switch and for a moment, the air brightened with the extra light.

Then the whole street plunged into darkness.

'Damn it,' Jack said, from the top of the ladder. 'We must have blown something.'

Holly felt her heart sink into her stomach. So much for the perfect Christmas surprise.

'Shall I check the fuse box?' She might not be a qualified electrician, but she'd learned a lot since becoming a home-owner. It wasn't like Sebastian had ever been any good at DIY or home maintenance, anyway.

'Hang on,' Jack said. 'I think it's going to take a bit more than that. Let me come down first. Hold the ladder?'

'Sure.' Holly stepped back over the low hedge into Kathleen's garden, and grabbed the ladder firmly. 'Okay, ready.'

As Jack began his descent in the darkness, Holly realised that people were already coming out of their houses, carrying torches, trying to figure out what was going on. Her stomach swirled with rising panic. Oh God, this was all their fault. And any moment now, Kathleen would come out too, and the whole Christmas surprise would be ruined. All this work for nothing.

Why was nothing going right this week? First they'd lost Claude, now they'd screwed up Christmas.

Just then, as if he'd heard his name in her thoughts, a small, compact dog came bursting out from the hedge between the two houses, followed by – of all creatures Perdita, her tail bushier than ever. They must have been startled by the sudden darkness, she realised.

'Claude!' she cried, and the little dog stopped.

'Claude's here?' Jack called, from halfway down the ladder.

'He just ran in!' Holly tried to bend down to Claude's level, without letting go of the ladder. It was harder than it sounded. 'Here, boy. Everything's okay now, Claude. We just want to make sure that you're somewhere safe for—'

At her words, Claude launched himself away from her at far greater speed than she'd imagined he was capable of. 'Claude!' she cried again, letting go of the ladder to try and catch him, but the little dog slipped through her fingers, racing forwards – and smacking straight into the ladder.

'What the—' Jack yelled. And then he wasn't saying anything at all.

Because then he was sprawled on the grass beside her as the ladder crashed down and hit the ground.

CHAPTER
FOURTEEN

CLAUDE

The sound of the ladder crashing down beside me sent me scurrying backwards in the darkness, and it took me a moment to realise that the groaning figure on the ground was Jack.

'Jack!' Holly rushed to his side, forgetting all about me.

I should run. This was my chance to get away, while no one could see anything. It might be the only way to avoid the pound – because there wasn't a chance they weren't going to send me there now.

I'd made Jack fall.

I'd hurt Jack.

'What are you still doing here?' Perdita scampered up to my side, her fur bushier than ever. 'Run now, you idiot! Or else you're in big trouble!'

She was right – they didn't give you a pat and some gingerbread and say 'Good dog' when you'd done something like this. And they weren't even my humans. They had no reason to forgive me.

But I couldn't make my paws leave the ground. Not with Holly's scream still echoing in my ears. Not when Jack was hurt and it was my fault.

'I'm okay,' I heard Jack say, but he groaned again as he tried to sit up. 'What happened?'

People were filling the garden now from all the houses on Maple Drive, shining torches ahead of them, coming to see what had happened, if Jack was okay. The rest of the lights were still out, and in the darkness it was hard to make out anybody's faces, to tell who was a friend and who wasn't.

But I was still Jack's friend, even if he didn't know it.

'I'm so sorry!' Holly sobbed, on her knees beside Jack. 'I let go of the ladder to try and catch Claude, but he escaped and crashed into it.'

Holly was blaming herself? I couldn't have that. Not when it was so clearly all my fault.

No wonder Daisy and Oliver had left me behind. Who knew what trouble I could have caused them with France, ferry and chateau.

But Jack and Holly were still here. And I had to make this up to them, somehow – or at least show them how sorry I was.

Nudging my way past the people gathering around, and skipping over the rungs of the ladder, I made my way to Jack's side, nuzzling at his hand until he rubbed between my ears.

'Hey Claude, buddy,' he said, struggling to sit up. 'You came home.'

Claude's back. The whisper went up through the crowd, the news passing backwards until my name seemed to fill Maple Drive. Everyone knew who I was – and now they knew what I'd done.

I whimpered, hoping against hope that Jack would be okay. That he'd really forgive me, once he realised what had happened.

'You shouldn't sit,' Holly admonished, pushing on his shoulders until he lay down again. 'You need a doctor.'

'Where's Dr Roberts?' someone in the crowd asked. 'From number 2?'

'He's just putting his shoes on,' someone else answered. 'Here he comes.'

'I'm fine, really,' Jack said. 'Had far worse bangs to the head than this in my time.'

I whined, sad at the thought of Jack being hurt, and he wrapped a hand around my middle, pulling me closer. 'No more running off, you,' he murmured to me. 'You stay with Holly and I'll find you some gingerbread once they let me up again, okay? We're going to get you home soon, I promise.'

Jack's promise sent a warm feeling through me – the kind of 'home' feeling that I hadn't felt since Daisy and Oliver drove away.

Could things really be okay?

Then the doctor was there, examining the bump on Jack's head. Holly scooped me up into my arms and held me close. 'We were so worried about you, Claude. Why didn't you trust us? We're your friends.'

I wanted to explain – wanted to tell her I knew about the pound, that I'd been scared. But now … if they weren't sending me away now, when I'd hurt Jack, maybe I really could trust them. Maybe I was home, after all.

Kathleen's front door opened at last. It seemed like days since I'd tried to get her attention through the window, and longer since I'd sat in her kitchen and had my first taste of gingerbread. So much had happened since then.

'What on earth is happening out here?' she asked, from her front step.

'I'm so sorry, Kathleen,' Holly said, carrying me closer. I wriggled a little until she put me down, then curled up on her feet. I wasn't going anywhere until I knew that Jack was *definitely* okay. Doctors, I knew, were like human vets. I wanted to hear him say Jack was all right. 'We were trying to organise a Christmas surprise for you. And, well, for ourselves, too. We decorated the whole street with lights, but then the power blew, and Jack fell … and now everything's ruined.'

'A Christmas surprise?' Kathleen said, sounding astonished. 'For me?'

'I'm so sorry we messed it up.'

'Darling, just the idea that you thought of me, at such a busy time of year …' She reached over and kissed Holly on the cheek. 'Bless you, my dear. Bless you.'

'Well, I don't think there's any permanent damage,' Dr Roberts said, getting to his feet from where he'd been kneeled beside Jack. 'But I'll want to keep an eye on you for a day or so, and absolutely *no ladders*. Okay?'

'Yes, sir.' Jack sat up again and, this time, everyone let him. A man reached out a hand to help him to his feet. 'Now, how about we get some lights back on around here, hey?'

'Already on it,' someone else called, from over by Holly's house. 'My brother works for the electric company. He'll get someone out here as quick as can be and we'll have power again in no time.'

I shifted over to lean against Jack's leg, just to check he was really fine. That I hadn't hurt him too badly.

And yes, okay, to remind him I was still there, and that he'd promised me gingerbread.

'Come on then,' Jack said. 'We've still got a lot to do before tomorrow. And I *did* promise Claude some gingerbread.'

I barked my approval at that, and Holly laughed. 'Of course he's learnt that word.'

She turned, Jack at her side, me at their feet, to make her way through the crowd to her own house. She almost made it, too.

But then, all conversation stopped, as the thundering voice of Mrs Templeton cut through the night.

'*What the devil is going on here?*'

DAISY

It was nearly midnight before Daisy and Oliver returned to the hotel. Feeling fuzzy after several glasses of very lovely wine, Daisy clung to Oliver's arm and buried her head against his shoulder to protect against the bitter French cold as they made their way back.

Christmas, Daisy had decided, might not be a total disaster after all. They were all together, she'd had a lovely night out with her husband for the first time in over a year, and now she got to spend the night in a nice hotel before travelling home to Claude in the morning. The kind hotel owners had even let them put the perishables from their M&S hamper in the fridge, so there was an outside chance the smoked salmon might still be good tomorrow. The turkey they'd left in the fridge at the chateau. There were limits to how many food miles Daisy was willing to chalk up for her Christmas dinner.

No, all in all, things could be a lot worse. Really, far, far—

'Oh bollocks,' she said, coming to a sudden stop in the middle of the road.

'Oh hell,' Oliver said, stopping with her. 'What now?'

'Bloody Santa Claus.' How could she have forgotten the most important job she had on Christmas Eve? Santa needed his parent-elves after all. And Jay would never understand if

Father Christmas didn't arrive for them all tonight.

Oliver groaned. 'Maybe he couldn't find us. Maybe he's left all the presents ready for us back at Maple Drive.'

'Yeah, because that's going to work with Jay.' Daisy sighed. 'No, there's nothing for it. We're going to have to go fetch all the presents from the car and break into their room.'

'Without waking Jay or Bella,' Oliver said, sceptically. 'Somehow that seems less likely than the Maple Drive thing.'

'I know.' Jay was a notoriously light sleeper. There was no way they'd manage it.

'Maybe the stockings could be hung on the door handle? Outside the room?' Oliver suggested.

'That could work. I'd just put them in our room, but you remember what happened last year.'

'All too well.' Oliver shuddered. Apparently Jay bursting into their room at four-thirty in the morning, bouncing onto the bed and landing on a very sensitive part of Oliver's anatomy had permanently traumatised her husband.

'I mean, he's unlikely to have an aim *that* perfect two years running,' Daisy said. 'But if he comes present hunting in our room and wakes the twins before they're ready, *nobody* is going to be having a perfect Christmas.' Not to mention the fact that it was probably bad form to start drinking before sunrise on Christmas Day. And if things went at all like last year, it was a very real possibility for both of them. And one of them had to drive them all home.

'So, presents in the kids' room,' Oliver agreed, hurriedly.

Daisy nodded. 'At least that way there's a stack of interesting stocking fillers that might keep Jay going until sunrise. We just need to haul them all in to the hotel.'

'Better make a start, then,' Oliver said, reaching into his

pocket for his car keys as they reached the hotel car park.

As she and Oliver struggled to carry the twins' ridiculously large present between them, up the three flights of stairs to their hotel rooms, Daisy reflected that maybe Santa could have just delivered to the car. That would have been a hell of a lot easier, even if it had resulted in Oliver getting bashed in the boy parts again.

'How were they?' Daisy asked her mother, in hushed tones, as they stepped out into the hallway to discuss, hoping the extra door between them would stop the twins waking up. Oliver pointed towards the stairs and headed back for another load of presents.

'Little angels,' Mum said, which sounded utterly unlike her children to Daisy, but she decided to go with it.

'Are Jay and Bella asleep?' God, she hoped so. If she had to sit up and wait for Jay's excitement levels to finally subside far enough for him to pass out, she couldn't promise she wouldn't be snoring long before Santa had been.

'I think so. I stuck my head in an hour or so ago, and Jay was flat out. Bella still had her headphones on, but I took them off. They're both fine,' Mum reassured her.

'Brilliant,' Daisy said, with a sigh of relief. 'Thanks, Mum.'

Mum smiled. 'Did you have a lovely time?'

'We did, thanks. It was nice to, well, just be us for a change.'

Mum's smile turned a little sad. 'And to think, that's just what your father and I were trying to avoid.'

'Do you think you're going to keep the chateau?' Daisy asked, wine making her blunt.

'Maybe. It would make a very nice holiday rental, after all …'

'For birdwatchers, maybe,' Daisy said.

Mum snorted a laugh, covering her mouth with a hand to try and keep the noise in, so as not to disturb the twins. Her eyes grew too wide, like keeping the laughter inside was straining her body. Daisy couldn't help it. She collapsed into giggles, putting one hand out against the hideous rose covered wallpaper to keep herself upright as the laughter overtook her, heaving in huge breaths in between.

'When … when your dad …' Mum said, unable to get the words out between silent laughs. 'When the bird pooed on his head!'

'I know!' Daisy fell apart all over again. 'And when … when he tried to catch it in the saucepan!'

Mum bent over in the middle, one arm wrapped around her stomach as if her laughter had grown physically painful. 'I'd never heard him use some of those words before!'

'His French swearing is actually pretty impressive,' Daisy said, in between bursts of laughter.

Oliver appeared at the top of the stairs behind them, another bag of presents in his hands, and surveyed the scene. 'What's so funny?'

'Dad,' Daisy managed. 'And the bird. We should … Oh God, we should buy him birdwatching binoculars for his birthday!'

Mum howled with laughter at that, but Oliver just rolled his eyes.

'Let's get through Christmas first, shall we?' he suggested, good humouredly. 'Come on, elves. Santa needs a little help.'

'Okay, okay.' Daisy straightened up, wiping her eyes to clear them of tears of laughter.

'But your dad *definitely* needs a new saucepan,' Mum said, and Daisy gave up the struggle and leant against the wall and laughed and laughed.

Oliver sighed. 'Father Christmas never had this sort of trouble,' he said. But he didn't look cross. In fact, Daisy thought, as she watched him through her giggles, he looked more like the man she'd married than ever.

And for the first time since the twins were born, she was starting to feel like the woman he'd married, too.

HOLLY

Somehow, despite all the torches shining on her, the night seemed dark again. Holly felt Jack's hand in hers and hoped that it would give her the strength to stand up for what she wanted, and say what needed to be said to Mrs Templeton.

She'd been *so sure* they'd had a breakthrough with the woman that afternoon. After all their talk about community, after asking her to be involved in the Christmas surprise, she'd really hoped that Mrs Templeton would be on their side now. That they were bringing Maple Drive together, not causing more division in place of the indifference that had been fostered there before.

But from the look on Mrs Templeton's face, she was wrong.

Arms folded across her chest, holding her red brocade dressing gown closed over her nightdress, Mrs Templeton tapped her slipper on the grass and scowled under her iron grey hair.

'I'll ask again,' she said, when no one answered. 'What, exactly, is going on here? And why, as Neighbourhood Watch Warden, did nobody wake me when the lights went out? I'd never have known at all if it wasn't for all the noise out here.'

'We're sorry, Mrs Templeton,' Jack said, rubbing the back of his head as he spoke. It had to hurt, Holly was sure. She shivered a little at the thought of how close he'd come to being seriously injured. 'We were hoping to make this a surprise.'

Mrs Templeton took a moment to look around, surveying the lights failing to illuminate the street. In the torchlight, the dark outlines of the shapes looked sad and lonely. Holly looked with her, wincing a little as she wondered how the woman who'd hated her elegant icicle lights was going to feel about the Rudolph on the roof of number 3, once they got it lit again.

'It most certainly is that,' Mrs Templeton said, faintly. 'I notice you haven't thought to affix any lights to *my* house.'

Holly and Jack exchanged a look. Was she hoping they *would*? Or was she warning them off? It was kind of hard to tell.

'Your house was next on our list,' Holly said, taking a chance. 'Although, obviously we'd have asked your permission first.'

'Of course.' Mrs Templeton gave a regal nod. 'I suppose I could bear to live with some of those snowflake lights. Just to make sure the whole street is in harmony.'

'I'll get them up for you now,' Jack said, beaming.

'Oh no you won't.' Dr Roberts bustled through the crowd to object. 'You're not going anywhere near a ladder, remember? You're sitting down and recovering. I'm sure there are plenty of people here willing to help out.'

A murmur went through the neighbours, and Jessica from number 3 put herself forward for the job.

'Right then,' said Mrs Templeton, rubbing her hands together. 'Now that's sorted – or will be once the power's back on – what's next? I can't believe that the lights were your *only* plan for a surprise Christmas for the street?'

For the street? When this had started, it had just been for Kathleen, and maybe for themselves. Then that had grown to include Mrs Templeton, and now … everyone on Maple Drive. How had this happened?

And why couldn't she stop smiling at the idea?

The crowd was silent, waiting to hear her reply. 'Um, well, the plan was really still a work in progress,' Holly admitted, still grinning.

Mrs Templeton rolled her eyes. 'Honestly. Amateurs. Lucky for you I've organised a fête or two in my time. I know *just* what we need to do. Starting by getting inside where we can discuss the plan and allocate jobs.'

Never mind that it was nearly midnight. Never mind that her house wasn't big enough to fit everyone in, and she'd have to light candles everywhere just to be able to see anyone. Never mind that Claude was still curled up by her feet and would clearly need a place to stay for the night. And never mind that she'd never even spoken to half the people currently congregating on the street outside her house.

'Come on in, everyone,' Holly said, happily. 'I hope you all like mince pies!'

JACK

Jack, his head still banging, trailed into Holly's house behind the crowd, Claude at his feet. Perhaps this was all some sort of concussion-induced dream. It made a hell of a lot more sense than Holly suddenly accommodating the entire neighbourhood, for mulled wine and mince pies by candlelight at midnight on Christmas Eve.

'I've updated the Find Claude page,' Jessica, from number 3, told Jack as they squeezed through the front door. 'The McCawleys probably won't see it until morning, but I've told them that Claude is safe with you again now. I'll try and send a photo too, so they can see that he's okay.'

'Thanks,' Jack said. Just remembering that Claude was home made his head hurt less – even if the little dog was at least partially responsible for his accident. Jack didn't care.

Mrs Templeton quickly took charge of the gathering, while Holly hunted out glasses and mugs for the mulled wine.

'There'll be jobs for everyone in the morning,' Mrs Templeton said, her voice crisp as she surveyed the mass of people crammed into the house. She shook her head. 'But for now, we just need to plan, so most of you might as well go home and get some sleep.' There were a few objections to that, so Holly added, 'After you've had some mulled wine, and maybe some of my mince pies, of course.'

'But it's Christmas Day tomorrow,' Mrs Hodgkins from number 1 said, frowning. 'We can't just give up all our own plans and traditions for yours.'

'Of course not,' Holly said, soothingly. 'And we'd never ask anybody to. But if anyone is alone this Christmas, or looking for a little more company, we'd love to have you as part of our community Christmas, that's all. I mean, we'll just be right here in Maple Drive, so you can just pop out for half an hour, if you like. And nobody *has* to do anything. Right, Mrs Templeton?'

Mrs Templeton looked considerably less certain of that fact, but Jack suspected that came from decades of ordering people around as a headmistress.

'Holly's right,' he said, sensing she might need a little back-up. 'A community is only a community if everyone *wants* to be there, and wants to take part. We'd love to see all of you tomorrow, and celebrate Christmas with you. But we understand completely if you have other commitments, or choose not to join in.'

That calmed the crowd a little – or possibly that was just the effect of Holly's mulled wine.

Jack glanced around the kitchen, taking in the scene. People were spilling out through the back door, and into the hallway, and there were a few sitting down in the lounge, having the conversation relayed to them in a weirdly festive version of Chinese whispers. Claude, he noticed, was making the rounds of the kitchen, gobbling down all the scraps of gingerbread and pastry that people could feed him. Someone had put a pair of reindeer antlers on his head, but Claude didn't seem to mind. He'd probably never had his ears scratched by so many people before, Jack thought. And every one of them seemed honestly pleased to see him back where he belonged and safe. The antlers were probably a small price to pay.

Imagine, just a day ago, he'd believed that there was no community in Maple Drive, no Christmas spirit. And now the entire street was planning a Christmas ... not a surprise for Kathleen. How could it be, when they were all in on it? A celebration of Christmas, and their community, perhaps.

Or maybe it didn't matter what it was called. Just that, against all the odds, it was happening.

Eventually, Mr Yates' brother showed up from the electric company, made some calls that Jack suspected wouldn't have been made for anyone else, and informed them all that the power would be back within an hour or two.

Once the mulled wine ran out, most people left, but by that time Mrs Templeton had a pretty good list going on the notepad she'd pulled from her dressing gown pocket when she sat down. People had volunteered food and services and help, and Mrs Templeton seemed to know what they'd all lead to, even if Jack wasn't sure at all.

Eventually, there was just Jack, Holly, Kathleen, Mrs Templeton and Claude left.

Jack took a seat at the table with the women, and didn't object when Claude climbed into his lap, his muzzle covered in crumbs. He felt warm and content and sleepy under Jack's hands as he removed the antlers he was wearing. He wondered if they'd ever know exactly what sort of adventures Claude had been having while he'd been away.

Whatever they were, he seemed grateful to be back amongst friends and gingerbread again. And Jack was very grateful to have him there.

'So, I think that's everything sorted.' Mrs Templeton underlined something on her list, then showed it to Kathleen and Holly, who both nodded.

'We'd better get some sleep,' Kathleen said, pushing her hands against the table to help her to her feet. 'Lots to do tomorrow.'

'Agreed.' Holly looked tired, Jack realised, but her eyes were still feverishly bright in the candlelight, from the excitement of the evening. He wondered if she'd sleep at all tonight.

'You look like I remember feeling as a child on Christmas Eve, waiting for the magic to happen,' he told her, as he pulled on his coat.

'Except we're not waiting for the magic,' Holly replied. 'We're making it.'

Jack grinned. He supposed she was right.

Leaving Claude snoozing in Perdita's cat basket, Jack walked the two older women back to their own homes. It was cold and dark and slippery out, and with them both in slippers and dressing gowns, he wasn't taking any chances of them falling and hurting themselves. There'd been enough of that for one night already.

As he headed back to Holly's, the whole street burst into light again, with snowmen and reindeer and icicles and snowflakes and Christmas trees shining down from almost every house in the street. He paused by the front door for a moment, and took in the display. Even Mrs Templeton's house had delicate snowflake lights hanging from each of the windows, now. The only dark patch was Number 11 – Claude's house.

'Do you think his family will be home in time for Christmas?' Holly asked from behind him, and he realised she was staring at the same thing he was.

'I hope so,' he said, thinking about the McCawleys, stranded in France, missing Claude.

'Me too,' Holly said. He turned towards her, and saw she had her arms wrapped around her middle to ward off the cold. Instinctively, he took her hand and tugged her towards him, so she stood with her back to his chest, and his arms around her waist.

'We'll look after him, though. If they don't,' he said, wanting to reassure her.

'I know. But ...' she sighed. 'I know what it feels like to be abandoned. I wouldn't want that for Claude. He can't understand that they're trying to get back to him. All he knows is that he's alone.'

'But he's not, is he?' Jack said, suspecting they weren't just talking about Claude any more. After all, the little dog wasn't the only one who'd been left behind this Christmas. Holly should have been married to that idiot Sebastian by now – a thought that Jack hated even thinking. 'He's found new friends – us for a start. New people who love him just as much. Who won't ever leave him.'

Holly froze in his arms, and he knew that she had read the hidden meaning in his words. 'Perhaps,' she said. 'But then, how can you ever really be sure that someone will stay? I mean, things change, don't they? A new opportunity. A new job ... and suddenly people leave you.'

'I suppose so,' Jack admitted. Maybe this wasn't just about Sebastian, either, he realised. Hadn't Jack told her that he'd applied for a transfer? And yes, things had changed since then. And yes, maybe he did want to stay in Maple Drive, after all – if everything worked out the way he hoped. But Holly didn't know that. She thought he was leaving – and he wasn't a hundred per cent sure she even wanted him to stay.

But he knew he had to take a chance that she did, or he'd regret it forever.

Just telling Holly he planned to stay wouldn't be enough. She'd been let down and left behind once too often before.

He had to prove it to her.

And standing there, watching the lights of Maple Drive twinkling in the darkness, he knew exactly how.

CHAPTER FIFTEEN

CLAUDE

'Well, look at you two sweethearts.' Holly's voice cut through the fog of sleep still surrounding me, and I stirred, trying to find wakefulness. I was curled up against something else furry, and soft. Fluffy, in fact ... Hang on, was I in Perdita's bed with her? I had a vague memory of falling asleep there.

Oh, who cared? I was warm and cosy, and for the first time in days I'd actually slept well enough to feel rested. In fact, my stomach was rumbling again, I'd been asleep so long. 'Merry Christmas, both of you! There's special breakfast for you both when you get up.'

Breakfast. In fact, *special* breakfast.

Suddenly my eyes were wide open.

Holly laughed. 'I knew that would get you moving. Come on! It's a busy, busy Christmas Day!'

Music played from the stereo on the kitchen counter, and Holly sang along as she put cat food into Perdita's bowl, and something else from a tin into a second bowl she pulled from the cupboard. 'A special donation from one of our neighbours,' she explained as she spooned the food in. It looked moist and juicy and meaty and *delicious*. 'Mr Yates at number 6 was worried that you might be a little peckish, and not so keen on cat food. He showed up just after sunrise with this for you.' She held up the blue tin. It had a picture on it of a dog who looked a little like me – although not as handsome, of course. 'Wasn't that kind of him?'

I showed my appreciation for Mr Yates' kindness by launching myself mouth first into the bowl. Oh, it was *good*.

There was a knock on the door, and Holly went to answer it, voices floating through the house – Christmas greetings and laughter and more music. Perdita prowled up to her bowl beside me. 'I suppose you think you're set for life now, then,' she said, sighing as she delicately bit into her first mouthful of food. But somehow, the old venom was missing from her voice.

I was starting to think that Perdita didn't mind having me around at all.

'Thank you for letting me share your bed last night,' I said, between chews. 'I appreciated it.'

Perdita tilted her head to look at me. 'You're welcome,' she said. 'This once. Just until your family come home.'

'Agreed.' Because surely Daisy and Oliver would be back soon. And then I could go home, for real.

Although I might still pay the occasional visit to Holly. And Jack. And Kathleen. Especially if any of them had gingerbread in.

Once I'd finished my breakfast, I padded out into the hallway to see what else was going on. Away from my food bowl, the air smelled crisp and cold – but with a hint of the sort of spices and flavours that had led me to discovering the wonders of gingerbread in the first place. People were everywhere; not just in the house, but out in the street, too, moving tables and chairs out from their houses into the road, and carrying plates and boxes from house to house, laughing and joking as they worked. The lights on the houses had been turned off for now, but the winter sun shining on the white and frosty ground more than made up for them. Everything looked bright and new and shiny.

And every person who saw me, as I trotted up and down the street, surveying the action, stopped to say, 'Hello, Claude,' and scratch my ears.

Maple Drive seemed a different place than the one Daisy and Oliver had driven away from, just two days ago.

And I had to say, I liked the *new* Maple Drive a whole lot better than the old one.

DAISY

'He's been! Mum, Dad! He's been!' Jay's voice resonated through the hotel room, and Daisy smiled as Oliver hid his head under the pillow with a groan. At the end of the bed, Lara and then Luca stirred in their travel cots, as Jay began hammering on the door.

'Merry Christmas, darling.' Daisy dropped a kiss onto Oliver's bare shoulder, then pulled on her dressing gown as she went to let her older children in.

'I tried to keep him in bed longer,' Bella said, her eyes tired. 'But he was desperate to come and see you, the moment he'd finished opening all the presents in his stocking.'

'That's okay,' Daisy said, hugging her daughter. 'Merry Christmas, Bell.' Behind her, she heard Oliver howl as Jay landed on the bed.

It was beginning to feel a lot like Christmas.

'Merry Christmas everyone!' Dad boomed from the doorway, a Santa hat lodged on his head at a jaunty angle.

'Any good children here waiting for presents?' Mum asked from behind him.

Soon, they were all piled into the one hotel room, Jay between Daisy and Oliver under the covers, Bella perched on the far end of the bed, Dad in the chair by the window and

Mum on the dressing table stool holding Lara. Luca nestled in Daisy's arms, and she suddenly couldn't remember how many times she'd been woken in the night to feed them, or how awful the explosive nappy change at 2 a.m. had been.

All that mattered was that her family were together, demolishing forests' worth of wrapping paper by the second as they ripped into their gifts.

They'd retrieved croissants and chocolate spread from the M&S hamper, since the hotel didn't start serving breakfast for another hour, and were tucking into them as they handed out presents. Daisy hoped that housekeeping staff were up to dealing with all the crumbs …

The twins seemed to like their special giant play nest, as well as playing Old MacDonald, filled with soft animals that made noises and had crinkly textures and plastic mirrors and chewable bits. Well, as much as two five-month-olds could really like anything. Still, it gave them somewhere to play while everyone else got on with opening their presents.

'Cool,' Bella said, as she opened the new headphones Daisy had scoured the internet for, after she mentioned them. Oliver opened a new cookery book, aimed at men, and gave Daisy a look.

'Is this a hint?'

Daisy widened her eyes. 'I think that one's from Santa, darling. Maybe *he* thinks you should cook more.'

'Hmm,' Oliver hummed, unconvinced. But he did open the book and start reading, which Daisy took as a small victory.

'Mum? This is for you.' Jay handed her a sloppily wrapped parcel with a glittery bow on the top. Oliver's wrapping skills, Daisy recognised.

'Thank you, darling.' She kissed Jay on the top of the head, then set about untangling the roll of Sellotape that had been wrapped around her present. Eventually, she made it inside, and pulled out a mug, covered in childish drawings and the words 'World's Best Mum' in bright red printed letters.

'That's us,' Jay explained, pointing to the stick figures. 'That's Dad, with the tie, and you with the beautiful hair. Then Bella, and me, and the twins – except I couldn't draw them very well, so I drew them in their pushchairs. And there's Claude.' His voice wobbled a little on his beloved pet's name.

Daisy held him closer. 'I love it. Thank you, Jay. It's the best present I've ever been given.'

'Don't know why I bothered with the spa voucher, then,' Oliver muttered, and she flashed him a grin.

'Okay, that was pretty good too.' Not the voucher itself, of course, but the implicit promise. One day, in the not-too-distant future, Oliver would have to take charge of all four kids, and the house, and the dog, for a full day, while she went somewhere relaxing and calming and did nothing for several hours.

Bliss.

'Right, last one,' Dad said, pulling another present from the bag. They all turned to look, and he pulled out a red velvet stocking, covered in embroidered bones.

'That's for Claude,' Jay said, and bit his lip.

Suddenly, the mood dropped again. Yes, it was lovely to have her family together on Christmas Day, Daisy realised, but there was still one thing missing.

Bella pulled her phone from her pyjama pockets. 'I've got one more Christmas present for you all,' she said, holding it up.

'What?' Jay asked, frowning. 'That's just your phone.'

'Look closer.'

They all huddled around the phone to look at the screen.

'That's Claude!' Jay yelped. Daisy peered closer, and saw an unfamiliar photo of their pet, wearing a headband with reindeer antlers on, with a plate of gingerbread snowmen in front of him. 'Where is he?'

'The postman and the woman at number 12 are looking after him,' Bella said, with a laugh. 'He's absolutely fine, and waiting for us to get home.'

'I was wrong. *That's* the best Christmas present ever,' Daisy said, relief washing over her. She checked her watch. 'Right, we've got an hour and a half before we need to be at the terminal for our train. What do you say we all get cleared up here, get dressed, pack up the car and go home?'

Jay cheered, and even Bella gave up a little whoop.

It was time to go home to Claude. Then Christmas could *really* begin.

JACK

Maple Drive was almost unrecognisable when Jack walked through it on Christmas morning. He'd overslept, just a little, after being so late home from Holly's, and after his fall. But apparently the rest of the community had been up and raring to go with the sun.

A long row of tables had been laid out down the middle of the street, and covered with a patchwork of table cloths in bright whites, reds, golds and greens. Bamboo canes had been affixed to the legs at regular intervals, and Mr Yates' fifteen-year-old son Toby was hanging tinsel and Holly's homemade bunting between them, helped out by another boy Jack didn't recognise from the street. Neighbours bustled past with table decorations, dishes, and in one case, a six-foot Christmas tree, already decorated. And in the middle of it all was Mrs Templeton, dressed now in a festive tartan skirt and thick red jumper, holding her notepad and directing the activities.

'Zach! Not another red piece of tinsel next to the green,' she called, to the boys hanging tinsel. 'Alternate!'

'Yes, Grandma,' said the boy Jack hadn't recognised. Well, that explained that, he supposed. He wondered if Mrs Templeton's family might decide to stay a little longer today, after all, once they took in all the festivity.

Despite all the people filling Maple Drive, Jack couldn't see the one person he was looking for: Holly.

Waving to people as he passed, Jack crossed over the road to Holly's house, and let himself in through the wide open door. He'd spent the walk over planning what he wanted to say to her, but now he worried she might not have the time to listen.

'Yes, the cake is ready to go out,' he heard her saying, before he even caught a glimpse of her. 'But be careful, the snowflakes are still drying on the top.'

'Understood.' Heather Roberts, the doctor's wife, stepped out of the kitchen with an immense Christmas cake in her arms – three tiers, perfect snowy white icing, snowflake decorations and a silver glitter sheen. Jack stared at it in awe as Heather walked past him heading outside. He'd known Holly was very talented, but that cake …

'You should be making cakes for a living,' he told her, as she stepped into the hallway, wiping her hands on her apron. She had flour on her nose, glitter in her hair, and Jack thought she'd never looked more beautiful.

'Maybe one day,' Holly said, her cheeks pink from the compliment. 'But I couldn't *just* make cakes. There are too many other things I like to make too.'

'And what would you do with all that air drying clay,' Jack said, straight faced, and Holly laughed, a beautiful, musical sound.

God, what would his army friends say if they could see him now, crazy for a girl he'd barely spent more than a day with, and planning on arranging his whole life around the possibility that she might want him too.

Actually, now he thought about it, he had a feeling that

they might be happy for him. And a little bit jealous, come to that.

Jack grinned, as he watched the cake taking centre position on the long table outside. Even from the distance of Holly's house, it looked stunning.

'You are a marvel,' he said.

'And you are late,' she replied. 'We've all been working for hours, you know.'

'I was looking for something,' Jack admitted, reaching into his pocket.

Holly turned to him, a curious look in her eye. 'Something for today? For the Maple Drive Christmas?'

'Sort of.' He pulled out the small box he'd found at the bottom of a rucksack he'd forgotten he'd owned, an hour or more after he started searching for it.

This was it. The moment he proved something to Holly. The moment his future could really begin.

All he had to do was hand her the box, and explain.

'Jack! We need you out here.' Kathleen stuck her head around the front door, and she grinned. 'Merry Christmas, by the way. But we need a little help before we can get to the celebrating.'

'Just one moment,' he started, but it was too late.

'Holly? Where do you want us to put Claude's gingerbread house?' Mrs Yates came bustling in past Kathleen, standing between him and Holly, and any hope of resurrecting the moment was gone. Jack stared at the gingerbread house, iced to perfection and laden with sweets he was fairly sure Claude shouldn't eat. But then he spotted the tiny black and white icing French Bulldog, sitting at the front door of the gingerbread house, and he smiled. It was perfect.

'Um, let's see if there's space on the extra table at the end,' Holly said, already following Mrs Yates back outside. 'I'll see you later, Jack?' she said, as she passed, and Jack nodded.

Apparently romance would have to wait. They had Christmas to pull off first.

'Come on then,' he said, to Kathleen. 'Where do you want me?'

CHAPTER
SIXTEEN

CLAUDE

By lunchtime, I had eaten gingerbread snowmen, another bowl of special dog food, and exchanged Christmas barks with at least three other dogs on the street. They'd all looked at me curiously, but it wasn't until I stopped to talk with Perdita that I understood why.

'Don't you see?' she asked. 'You're a legend in this street now. Without you, Jack would never have met Kathleen, so Jack and Holly would never have had the idea of holding a Maple Drive Christmas. And if you hadn't knocked over Jack's ladder last night … well, none of this might be happening at all.'

'But how do they all know about that?' I asked, confused. *I* certainly hadn't told them.

Perdita stuck her nose up in the air, almost as high as her tail. '*Some* animals gossip,' she said, as if that were a bad thing.

But then I realised; the only person who knew about all that was Perdita herself.

'Thanks, Perdita,' I called, as she stalked off towards where Holly was sitting with Jack, at the end of the table.

Perdita had made me a legend. She'd told my story, and the story had been retold around the neighbourhood, until everyone knew it. Maybe, in some small way, I'd brought the animals of Maple Drive together the way Jack and Holly had brought together the humans.

It was nice to think so, anyway.

Everyone was sat down at the long table in the middle of the street, loading their plates with all the different sorts of food that their neighbours had contributed to the feast. I made my way slowly from one end the table to the other, pausing by any likely looking hands that might pass me a scrap of turkey, or something even better. By the time I reached the far end of the table, up by my own house, I was *almost* full.

Well, I probably had room left for another gingerbread snowman, but that was about it.

I paused as I approached the head of the table; Mrs Templeton sat there, surveying the neighbourhood as a whole, as she always did. I'd heard Holly earlier, saying to someone how much nicer the old woman had turned out to be than she'd expected, but I didn't buy it. If anyone there was still likely to send me to the pound, I knew it was her.

Suddenly, as if she'd sensed my presence, she twisted in her chair and looked down at me, her face stern. I froze in place for a moment, wondering which way to run first.

Then, Mrs Templeton did something I'd never seen her do before. Ever.

She smiled.

'You're still here, are you?' she said. 'Well. I suppose we could come to a Christmas truce.' She patted her leg and I moved cautiously closer.

Then she picked up a gingerbread snowman from the table in front of her and held it out to me and I figured, if I could make friends with Perdita, my furry nemesis, what was one more enemy turned friend? So I jumped up into her lap to enjoy my treat.

The sound of metal clinking against glass cut through the chilly air, and the conversations around me stumbled to a halt as everyone turned to look at Jack, standing beside the table with all the desserts on it.

'Everyone? If I could just have a moment of your time,' Jack said. He looked a little awkward, standing there with everyone staring at him, but then Holly moved beside him, holding his hand, and he smiled again. 'I just wanted to thank you all for everything you've done to make the first Maple Drive Christmas a success.'

A cheer ran down the table and I barked my agreement.

'We couldn't have pulled this off without you,' Holly added. 'And it's been just brilliant.'

'It has,' Jack agreed. 'But there's one person who needs a very special thank you for making any of this possible. And that's our friend Claude.'

Me? I put my paws up on the table as all around me, the humans of Maple Drive burst into applause. Applause for me. Apparently it wasn't just the neighbourhood animals that thought I was a legend.

'If Claude hadn't belly-flopped his way into Holly's kitchen, we might never have become friends,' Jack went on. 'And if he hadn't broken into Kathleen's house, hunting for gingerbread, we'd never have had the idea for this Christmas celebration at all.'

'Don't forget the time capsule,' Holly added. 'It was Claude who found that, and brought Mrs Templeton into our plans.'

'Speaking of which,' Mrs Templeton said, 'I've put the time capsule tin at the end of the table, along with some paper, pens and envelopes. I thought it might be nice to start a new Maple Drive time capsule, in memory of the occasion.'

'What a lovely idea!' Holly beamed, her whole being happier than I'd ever seen her before. 'What do we need to do?'

'Just write down your favourite Christmas memory, or a Christmas wish, and put it in the tin. We'll bury it somewhere Claude can't find it, then dig it up again in, say, five years?'

'Sounds perfect,' Jack agreed. 'Which means there's just one thing left for me to do.' Reaching behind him, he picked up a plate from the dessert table, and walked towards me. My eyes widened as I realised what he was carrying. A whole *house* of gingerbread, with a little model of me at the front. 'Claude, this is for you, to say thank you for bringing us humans together this Christmas.'

'Just don't eat it all at once,' Holly warned, with a laugh.

I promised nothing. Suddenly I wasn't so full any more.

They'd made me a house of gingerbread. They'd talked about me like I was important – not just to my humans, but to everyone on Maple Drive. I knew now that, wherever Daisy and Oliver were, Maple Drive was where I belonged.

And I always, always would.

I barked with happiness, as Mrs Templeton broke off a small piece of the gingerbread roof for me to eat.

Everything seemed to be going perfectly.

Until the sound of an approaching car cut through the conversation, and everyone fell silent as we waited to see who had come calling.

But deep down inside, I already knew.

It was my family, at last.

DAISY

'Hang on, slow down,' Oliver cried, and Daisy instantly put her foot on the brake.

'What? Why ... Oh.' She slowed the car right to a halt, and stared through the windscreen at the road in front of her.

Was that really Maple Drive?

'What's going on?' Bella squeezed herself forward through the twins' car seats to try and get a look.

'I haven't the foggiest idea,' Daisy said, her voice faint.

For some reason, the entire population of Maple Drive seemed to be having dinner in the middle of the road. Wearing their coats, mostly. And there was a Christmas tree at the far end. And tinsel and bunting on sticks. And ... were those lights on the houses? They weren't turned on, so it was hard to tell in the daylight, but Daisy was pretty sure they were.

'We were only gone two days.' Oliver shook his head in amazement.

'Nobody mentioned this on the Find Claude page,' Bella said.

'Can you see Claude?' Jay called from the back seat, trying to push past his sister.

'Not yet,' Daisy said, soothingly. 'He's probably at the house, Jay. I wouldn't worry. Come on, we'll go and look.'

Sliding the car up to the kerb, she parked, watching in her rear-view mirror as her parents did the same just behind them.

Stepping out of the car was almost like stepping onto a movie set, one of those films they only showed at Christmas, where everyone came together in the end to celebrate something or somebody. Except Daisy and her family were late to the cinema, and they hadn't got a clue what had happened to cause this.

As they moved closer, people at the nearest end of the table stood up to welcome them, beckoning them closer and grabbing more chairs from who knew where to squeeze around the table.

'You're back!' A man with dark, neat hair and a welcoming smile approached them, hand out stretched. 'Claude will be so happy.'

Daisy took the man's hand, trying to place him. Wait, wasn't he the postman? Hadn't Bella said he'd found Claude?

'Is he here?' she asked in a rush. 'We've been trying to get back ever since we realised he wasn't with us, but the ferries were cancelled and then we couldn't catch a train back through the tunnel until this morning, so we ended up staying in Calais last night and ... sorry. Do you know where Claude is?'

Jay was at his side in an instant, at the sound of Claude's name, and Bella wasn't far behind him. Leaving Oliver and her parents to deal with the twins, Daisy looked up hopefully at the postman, who grinned.

'Of course! He's the guest of honour at today's festivities. And I should warn you, he's discovered a love of gingerbread. Look, there he is.' He pointed down the table, and Daisy followed his finger, casting her eye across the gathering until she saw him.

Those ridiculous, wonderful black ears. That white wrinkled face. Those warm eyes. Their Claude.

But why on earth was he sitting on Mrs Templeton's lap?

HOLLY

'Holly, this cake is just divine!' A tall blonde in a white coat and suede boots, who didn't look like she'd ever eaten cake in her life, cornered Holly by the dessert table, leaving Holly scrambling to figure out which house and family on Maple Drive she belonged to.

Maybe number 4? The … Welwoods, was it?

'Thank you,' she said, smiling graciously, because even though Mrs (possibly) Welwood was the third person in the last ten minutes to compliment her on her Christmas cake, the pleasure was still very real. And unexpected.

'You *must* make my husband's fortieth birthday cake this year,' the blonde went on. 'It's in March, so we've got some time. I'll put together some ideas for themes, and you can just let me have your price list when we know what we're looking at, okay?'

'Um, I'm sure that will be fine,' Holly said, wondering what on earth a person was supposed to charge for cakes. Normally she just made them for her friends and family who, if she was lucky, paid her back for the ingredients. An actual commission was outside her realm of experience.

'In fact,' Mrs Welwood went on, 'perhaps you can help me out with one or two other aspects of the party planning. Like the decorations – you're so wonderfully crafty, aren't you? And maybe the theme. I'm sure you must have a great imagination. So that would help you with the invitations and so on …'

'Mrs Welwood,' Holly said, praying that *was* actually her name. 'Are you asking me to organise your husband's fortieth birthday party for you?'

'Oh, yes please.' Her face collapsed into a relieved smile, and suddenly she didn't seem so tall and intimidating. 'And call me Sharon, won't you? The thing is, I don't have the faintest idea where to start, and you did such a wonderful job organising all this!'

'Well, Mrs Templeton did a lot of it …'

Sharon shook her head. 'No. We've all been watching you, making sure she didn't get carried away, bossing everyone about. *You're* the one who made all this a success. You and that *gorgeous* fella of yours …'

'I wouldn't say Jack's *mine* exactly,' Holly said, hoping Sharon would put the pinkness of her cheeks down to the cold. 'But really, I've never organised a party before. I'm sure I can manage the cake—'

'And I'm sure we can manage everything, together. I'll pay you, of course. And once it's the huge success I know it will be, I'm sure all my friends will be lining up to hire you too!'

Holly considered it. The extra money would be super useful for paying the mortgage – and making headway towards paying Sebastian back his half of the deposit. If she could do a few parties, plus her craft stuff, and start saving, she could own that house free and clear eventually. It really would be hers. Her home.

She looked up and down Maple Drive, and saw Jack leading the McCawleys towards where Claude was sitting with

Mrs Templeton. She saw Kathleen, regaling half the table with stories from her youth, her travels. And she realised, this was where she wanted to belong.

Maple Drive was home. And Sharon Welwood's party was the first step towards making sure it could never be taken away from her again.

'I'll do it,' she said.

Sharon clapped her hands together and grinned. 'Brilliant! I'll call you in the New Year and we'll get planning, yeah?'

'I'm looking forward to it already,' Holly said, surprised to find that she really was.

'Holly?' Kathleen beckoned her over, and Holly went, obediently. 'Rebecca here, from number 7, was just asking about your bunting, dear. She's looking for some for the new nursery. Do you take commissions at all?'

Holly looked at Rebecca, her pregnant stomach pressing up against the table, then glanced up at the string of Christmas bunting hung between the bamboo canes on the table. They were fun and quick to make, looked impressive, and she could do it in front of a telly in the evenings, when she was feeling lonely.

'I absolutely do,' she said. 'We'll sit down soon and talk about exactly what you want,' she added, talking directly to Rebecca. She hadn't met her before, but if she lived in Maple Drive then Holly was already predisposed to like her.

Rebecca beamed. 'Oh, that would be lovely! I haven't had much of a chance to get to know people on the street since we moved in, and it seems like you and Jack are the heart of Maple Drive! You two must come over for dinner sometime.'

'Brilliant,' Holly said, but something about the woman's words tugged at her heart. *You and Jack*. Except there wasn't a Holly and Jack, really, was there? They hadn't even kissed. She'd thought he might kiss her the night before, but he'd just smiled at her and waved from the doorway.

. And there was still a very strong chance that he'd be leaving, and soon.

Would Maple Drive still accept her as one of their own if Jack left? She hoped so.

No, wait. That was wrong.

She would *make* it so.

This was her home, her place, with or without Jack. And the people here admired her talents, wanted to get to know her better. They liked her, just as she was. Soon, she'd be able to use her hobbies to pay back Sebastian and earn her home back. And she would make the community she'd always been looking for here in Maple Drive, even if Jack *did* leave.

It was just … she really hoped he'd decide to stay.

CHAPTER SEVENTEEN

CLAUDE

I stared across the table at Daisy and Oliver, Bella and Jay, Granny pushing the twins in their double buggy and Grandad following with Petal on her lead. All walking towards me.

I didn't know what to do. My heart pounded too hard and too fast in my chest, and I felt like I might throw up the gingerbread I'd just eaten. A huge part of me just wanted to jump down and run to them, but another, even bigger part was too scared.

Scared that they weren't back to stay. Scared that they hadn't missed me like I'd missed them. Scared that they'd forget me again, the next time something interesting came along.

I knew I could survive without them now. I had other people, people who stayed, who fed me, who cared about me.

But I knew in my heart, the McCawleys would always be my *real* family.

I just wished I could believe that I was family to them.

'So, you made it home, then,' Mrs Templeton said, her hand still resting on my back as the others approached.

Daisy smiled, but she looked tired – more tired than I'd seen her since the twins were new, even. 'Finally, yes. We've been trying to get back to our Claude ever since we left!'

Was that true? My heart started to rise, until I could almost feel it in my throat.

Then Jay yelled, 'Claude!' and dashed towards me and, without even realising I had done it, I jumped down from Mrs Templeton's lap and raced to meet him half way.

The little boy's arms linked around my neck as he held me close, my front paws on his shoulders, pressing myself as close as I could. I was trembling, I realised – and so was Jay. Tears landed on my fur as he whispered, 'I missed you so much, Claude. We never meant to leave you, you know. We've been trying to get home to you ever since. It wasn't Christmas without you there with us.'

Suddenly, the last of my fears faded away, floating off into the frosty air as Bella and Oliver and Daisy all knelt down to pat me and pet me and tell me they loved me, too.

We were a family once more. And I knew in my heart that they'd never leave me behind again.

DAISY

As evening crept in on Maple Drive, Daisy sat back in the chair Jack had found for her, Jay curled up in her lap while the twins snoozed in their buggy beside her. On the floor, Claude was keeping her feet nice and toasty. Over by the Christmas tree, she could see Bella sitting with Zach Templeton, dipping her head and tucking her hair behind her ear, and she thought *Boys, already?* But that was a problem for another day. Another, less perfect day than this one.

Oliver dropped a kiss onto her hair, resting his hands on her shoulders as they listened to a collection of neighbours singing Christmas carols while Dr Roberts played along on someone's keyboard that had been dragged outside.

'Well. If we'd known Christmas in Maple Drive would be like *this*, we never would have insisted on you coming out to the chateau!' Daisy's mother dropped into an empty chair beside her. 'Your father's on his third plate of food, and I just had the *most* interesting conversation with one of your neighbours. Why didn't you tell us what we were missing out on?'

'Because we didn't know,' Daisy admitted. 'Maple Drive … it's never been like this before.'

'I honestly thought we had the wrong road when we arrived,'

Oliver said. 'I can't imagine what changed here this week to make this happen.'

'I think you can blame it all on Claude.' They all turned as a woman in a bright red coat spoke, smiling gently as she bent down to rub between Claude's ears. Claude perked up for a minute, then settled back down again. 'Sorry, I don't think we've really met yet. I'm Holly. I live across from you at number 12.'

'Lovely to meet you,' Daisy said, frowning. 'But how could *Claude* have made all this happen?'

Holly laughed. 'Oh, he's had *quite* the adventure while you've been away!'

Bella approached, Zach following behind looking besotted. 'It's true, Mum. Look! Jessica from number 3 videoed this from earlier and put it up on the Find Claude page.' She held up her phone so they could both see Jack the postman, talking about Claude and presenting him with a gingerbread house.

Oliver shook his head. 'I still don't understand. He's just one little dog!'

'Tell us about it?' Daisy asked. 'Please? Only … we've missed him dreadfully. It would be nice to know what he's been up to without us.'

With a nod, Holly took a seat beside them. 'I heard you were trying to get back to him, the whole time?'

'We were,' Daisy said. 'I can't believe we managed to leave him behind in the first place! We think he must have jumped out of his cage in the boot to chase a cat or something.'

'Probably my Perdita,' Holly admitted. 'But, you'll be amazed to hear, they're friends now!'

Oliver reached for his wine glass. 'Clearly, this is quite some story.'

'It is,' Holly agreed. 'And it all started when Claude squeezed his way through Perdita's cat flap and into my kitchen ...'

Daisy settled back in her chair, ready to listen. The sky was starting to darken, but the garden heaters that had been brought out were keeping everyone warm. She was with her family, with her community, and Claude was safe.

It was the perfect Christmas, after all.

JACK

It had been an almost perfect day.

Jack had heard from just about everyone there how much they'd enjoyed themselves, how they'd always wanted to get to know their neighbours better but hadn't known where to start. There was a feeling of hope filling Maple Drive that Christmas Day, and Jack liked to think he'd played a small part in helping that hope grow. They'd even had a smattering of snowflakes earlier – not enough to drive everyone indoors, but enough to add a frosty white coating to the hedges and shrubs of the front gardens of Maple Drive.

Even Claude had found his family again.

Yes, things were very nearly perfect.

But not quite. Not yet, anyway.

From his chair by the Christmas tree, he watched Holly talking to the McCawleys, her hands animated as she spoke. Was she telling them the story of Claude's adventures over the last couple of days? Probably. But he knew the woman he'd met two days ago wouldn't have had the confidence to walk over there and do that.

Holly had changed – and he was so proud of her that he could burst. She'd found her place in the community and he knew, whatever came her way next, she could handle it. He hoped she knew that.

Now he just hoped that she had a place for him in her community, too.

As Holly stood, still smiling, and said goodbye to the McCawleys, Jack took his chance to find out. Moving swiftly around the long table, he intercepted her before she could get collared by anyone else wanting to ask her about her cakes, or her decorations.

In his hurry, he found himself diving directly into her path, so she almost crashed into his chest.

'Hey,' he said, softly, as she looked up at him in surprise.

'Hey. I didn't see you there.'

'I've barely seen you all day,' Jack said, smiling so she knew he wasn't complaining. 'You're in high demand.'

Holly ducked her chin. 'I don't know why. You and Mrs Templeton did at least as much as I did – probably more!'

'But you're the one who made the idea come alive in the first place,' he pointed out. 'You knew what this community needed – what everyone here wanted. And you're the only one who managed to make it happen.'

'Well, me and Claude,' Holly said, smiling up at him.

'And Claude,' he allowed. 'Where is he, anyway?'

'Passed out in a gingerbread stupor at Daisy's feet,' Holly said. 'I've just been talking with them. They're nice people, you know. I hoped that they would be. That they didn't mean to leave Claude behind.'

'I was sure they didn't,' Jack said. 'Even before we found out about the whole Find Claude campaign. That little guy gets under your skin. It's hard not to love him, once you've met him. A bit like someone else I know.'

Holly looked up sharply, meeting his gaze. 'Oh?'

Jack took a deep breath. 'I wanted to talk with you earlier.'

'I remember.' Holly's shoulders tensed, and Jack tried to figure out why before he said anything else. Was she working up to letting him down gently? 'Is it about your transfer?' she asked, after a second. 'Do you know when you're leaving?'

'No!' Jack said, too loud, and people around them turned to look. Damn. Just what he didn't need – an audience. He sighed. Well, he was doing this, whether people were watching or not. 'That's what I wanted to tell you. I'm not going anywhere.'

'Yet,' Holly added. 'And that's okay. I mean, yes, I'd love it if you'd stay. But really, we've only known each other a couple of days, really. I wouldn't ask you to make such a big decision because of me. And it's fine. I realised today … Maple Drive is my home. It's where I want to be. And now, I think I can be. I think I can make a place here – even if you don't stay. I'll be fine.'

'That's good to know,' Jack said, smiling. 'But it doesn't change the fact that I want to be here, with you – with your craft supplies, your sparkly cat leads, your incredible cakes … and just you. Exactly the way you are. Trust me. I'm not going anywhere.'

This time, Holly seemed to take the words in a little more, narrowing her eyes as she stared up at him. 'You're … not? Are you sure?'

'Very.' Jack wrapped an arm around her waist and pulled her even closer. 'But I get that it might be hard for you to believe that. Especially on two days' acquaintance. So I wanted to give you something, to show you I mean it.' He reached into his pocket and pulled out the box again.

Holly's eyes widened dramatically. 'Jack, really, it's okay. I believe you. You don't have to do anything extreme—'

'Calm down,' he told her, and flipped the lid open, revealing the necklace – a delicate silver chain with a tiny silver snowflake hanging from it, studded with specks of sparkling diamonds that looked like ice.

'Oh …' Holly reached out to touch it, then pulled her fingers away as a real snowflake landed on it. 'It's beautiful.'

'It was my mother's,' Jack explained, ignoring the flakes of snow as they started to fall again. 'She loved winter more than any other season, and Christmas most of all, so one year my dad gave her this necklace. And now I'm giving it to you.'

Holly looked up at him, horrified, and Jack worried for a second that he'd done this all wrong. Was this morbid? Or just crazy? Or—

'I can't take something so precious, Jack! It was your *mother's*.'

Ah. That made more sense. But fortunately he had the perfect answer.

'Then how about you just look after it for me,' he suggested. 'I mean, it's not like I'm going to wear it, right?'

He took the necklace from the box and fastened it around her neck, holding on a moment too long as he watched the snow fall around them, sparkling as it landed in her hair.

'Look after it?' Holly blinked away another snowflake. The snow was getting heavier, but Jack didn't care. He'd rather freeze out here with Holly than move anywhere.

'Yes. And if I ever leave, you can give it back to me,' he suggested. 'But I'm telling you now, there is nowhere I would rather see that necklace than around your neck.'

Holly's cheeks flushed a pretty pink colour. 'Yeah? Then I guess you'd better stick around to see it, then.'

'I guess I better had.' They smiled at each other for a long, long moment, and Jack could feel himself losing his mind in her blue eyes, until someone in the crowd yelled, 'Kiss her, you idiot,' and he realised that the snow hadn't driven anyone else inside either. The whole of Maple Drive was watching, and Jack didn't care at all. They were his new community, his new family, after all. Them and Holly, always. He'd found exactly what he'd been looking for all along.

As Jack bent his head to touch his lips to Holly's, someone flipped the switch he'd set up earlier. And when they kissed, every light and decoration in Maple Drive lit up, illuminating the night, and the street party, and all their new friends and old neighbours.

And as he held Holly close, Jack knew that his life would never be dark again.

EPILOGUE

CLAUDE

My home was just as I had left it.

As Daisy and Oliver put the children to bed, I curled up in my basket underneath the Christmas tree, enjoying all the familiar smells and sounds I'd missed over the last two days, and wondering what there might be for breakfast tomorrow.

Perhaps a really nice tin of dog food. To be honest, even I was getting a little sick of gingerbread.

But it didn't much matter what breakfast *was*, just that I got to eat it here, in my home, with my family.

I heard Bella calling goodnight and, over the baby monitor, Daisy singing a lullaby to the twins. Something about a silent night, which seemed a little optimistic.

I snuggled down, ready to rest myself. It had been a long day. Outside, the snow was still falling, and the Christmas lights Holly and Jack had put up sparkled in the darkness. It made me happy, just knowing they were there – and that I was inside in the warm, where I belonged.

On the stairs, a floorboard creaked, and a moment later, I heard the door into the lounge open. I lifted one eyelid to check for intruders, and then opened the other one too, when I saw it was Jay.

Kneeling beside my basket, Jay tucked his soft toy French

bulldog in beside me, and kissed me between my ears.

'Goodnight, Claude,' he whispered. 'Merry Christmas.'

Then Oliver called him upstairs to brush his teeth, and Jay scampered off again, leaving the toy with me.

I sighed a doggy sigh, snuggled up against the cuddly toy, and fell asleep, a very happy dog indeed.

Acknowledgements

As with every book I write, I owe a million thank yous to everyone who put up with me during the process. In this case, particular thanks goes to:

My Mum, for coming and looking after us every time one of us got ill (which was surprisingly often this year!).

My Dad, for manfully coping without Mum during those times. Also, and even more vitally, the new MacBook I used to write the story.

My husband, Simon, for constant support, care and general wonderfulness. Also pouring me wine, doing the laundry, and listening to me read out my pros and cons lists every time I have to make a decision about anything.

My daughter, Holly, for making the world a far more interesting place, and being very patient with me. (See, sweetheart, I told you I'd write a book with a Holly in it one day!)

My son, Sam, for being the most delightful baby boy ever, even when he brought home every possible cold, cough and stomach bug from nursery for four long months. Also, thank you for finally sleeping through the night. Your father and I appreciate it.

My agent, Gemma Cooper, for never saying 'I told you so' even when she totally could have, and for always responding to 84 panicked emails before breakfast with a calm and soothing phone call.

My editor, Charlotte Ledger, for cheering me on, supporting me and encouraging my career ever since that first cup of tea back in 2012. I'm still so thrilled, every single time we get to work together.